TEMPTED HERO

RETRIBUTION GAMES BOOK 3

ELLA MILES

RETRIBUTION GAMES SERIES

Mistaken Hero
Forbidden Princess
Tempted Hero
Fatal Princess
Tortured Hero
Dangerous Princess

PROLOGUE

RI

HE'S GOING to drop me.

I squeeze my eyes shut, preparing to be dropped, for it all to end. My eyes close before I realize that's not how I want to die—afraid and closed off from the world.

I look down at the rocks below being smashed by powerful ocean waves. The blue sea seems endless. It's beautiful. The sun is even setting and starting to streak orange and red colors across the clear sky.

I smile. If I'm going to die, then this is what I want to be my last memory. My last thought should be beautiful, not fearful.

Kek's dark laughter interrupts my beautiful exit, his hand strangling my neck. My feet are dangling over the cliff, scrambling, reaching for solid ground that isn't there. One slip of his hand and I'm gone.

I'm at peace with that.

Kek's cackle ruins my peace, though. I turn my head, glaring at the boy holding me. He's maybe five years older, but he's still a boy, still young. And yet, he already knows who he is. He's always known, while I'm still trying to figure out myself.

But I guess when your parents name you Kek—after the god of darkness—you don't really have much say in who you're going to be. His mother named him that because he was born in the dead of night under a moonless, starless sky. With his jet black hair, it made perfect sense to name him the god of darkness. She didn't realize how dark his soul would become as well.

"You can still save yourself, Princess. Trade your life for hers. Just say the word," Kek says.

Every time he's taken me, it's always the same. He pushes me to my limits, seeing how much pain and torture I can endure, and promises me it will end if I give her up, trade my life for hers.

Her.

I'd do anything for her.

I'd do everything for her.

That's never going to change.

This monster has come in and out of my life so many times to play his stupid games. I'd do almost anything to escape him, except give him her.

"No. Kill me," I say, glad this is the final time. After this, I won't have to see him ever again. No one will be left to protect her, although he doesn't know where she is. That will keep her safe.

He clucks his tongue. "Oh, sweet, foolish Princess. This drop won't kill you."

I look down at the rough rocks. It sure as hell looks like I'll die.

"It will," I say, more assured of myself.

"It won't. Want to know how I know?"

I shake my head—more games.

"You're a fighter. You won't give up. You can pretend you want to die all you want, but you won't. The rocks will break open your skin, and you'll lose a lot of blood. Maybe you'll even lose consciousness, but then you'll fight. Fight to live. To protect. To save. That's who you are, Rialta. A fighter. A princess."

I shake my head, hating all of his words.

He pets my hair, making me wince.

"You can be both a princess and fighter."

"I don't want to be a princess anymore."

He smiles. "Someday, you won't be."

Yea, when I'm dead.

I sigh and close my eyes, deciding I was right the first time. It's better if my eyes are closed.

And then he drops me.

My mind goes to her.

The last time I saw her was a couple of years ago. We were playing on the beach, running up and down it. There was a boy chasing after her. There were always boys chasing her, even at a young age. She may have not been a princess like me, but she would have made a perfect princess. She was sweet and kind and perfect. She loved dressing up in pretty dresses. She liked makeup and boys and being doted on.

The boys would use sticks to do fake sword fights to win her. She loved it, while I'd rather be fighting than waiting for one of them to win me.

This boy wanted her. He wanted all of her attention. But I was only visiting for a short time. I wanted her attention. So I fought him. I won. He looked so devastated that I let him spend time with us.

He would hold her hand. He kissed her cheek. He looked at her like he loved her.

I smiled. She would get her happily ever after. She would find a boy like this one who would love her forever.

My feet hit the water; the memory knocked from my head as I jostle along the rocks and plunge further into the water. I kick and kick, finally reaching the surface. I take a deep breath—hating that I'm breathing.

Kek was right.

I survived. I'm a fighter.

Only later would I realize that it was all for nothing. I couldn't save her—the caring, innocent girl who deserved to be a princess.

Kek found her.

He killed her.

And I'll never be the same again.

1

RI

Caius is safe.

Beckett is safe.

Gage, Hayes, and Lennox are safe, at least for now.

I gave up everything for Caius. I played almost every card I have in order to keep him safe from my father. I'm not sure what I have left to protect Beckett from any future attacks, but I'll give up what little leverage I have left. I would give everything in life I have, every other thing I love—anything for Beckett. I'd give everything and more, so much more.

I just hope I never have to. Caius protected Beckett. I protected Caius. And now that I'm no longer forbidden, Vincent can't use Beckett fucking me against him. I'm not sure if Beckett ever will sleep with me again, but I'll trade having to fend off the thirty contestants remaining if I can fuck Beckett without risking his life.

"You're dismissed. The next games are tomorrow at nine PM," Vincent says.

I don't look at him, nod, or give him any indication that I heard him speak. I walk out of the room.

I consider going back to my apartment with Lucy. I'd love to see her, and my guards Adrian and Georgio would allow it, but the memories of Beckett are too strong. I'm barely keeping everything together as it is. If I went back to the place Beckett fucked me, all those memories would overwhelm me. I'd never recover. I'd cry all night.

Instead, I walk upstairs to the bedroom Vincent still keeps for me. My childhood bedroom feels more like a fairytale tower, except my life is more twisted tragedy than an actual fairytale.

I hear Georgio and Adrian following behind me as I make my way upstairs. "Is this really necessary? I'm in Vincent's condo. It's secure. Do you really need to follow me around and stand guard outside my door?"

"You know we do," Georgio says too happily.

I look over my shoulder and I realize he's staring at my ass in my silk dress.

I stop abruptly and elbow him hard in the nose to explode spurts of blood from his face.

Adrian laughs full out.

"What was that for?" Georgio says between moans, acting like he's dying.

"That was for staring at my ass. Don't do it again."

"I wasn't—"

I glare at him.

"Okay, okay, okay. I was. I won't again. Corsi should know—"

"That you got your ass kicked by a girl? Go ahead and tell him," I say.

Then I sprint to my bedroom and shut the door, so I don't have to listen to Georgio tell me how unfair it is that I can hit him, but he can't hit me back. *He wants to talk about fairness?* He should trade places with me; then he'll know unfairness.

I kick off my heels, so tired of walking in the damn things. I'm unhooking my earrings that no longer put me in contact with the guys when I see a note lying on my bed addressed to Princess.

My heart beats once, twice, then flutters against my ribcage as fast as a hummingbird's wings.

Beckett?

The guys?

Did they somehow sneak in and leave me this note?

I glance around the room but don't see any signs of a break-in. We are on the top floor of a massive skyscraper. I can't imagine how they could get in, but I don't care. I just want their words. I want Beckett's words. I want his comfort, his love, his snark. I want all of it.

I dive onto the bed, scooping up the letter like a teenager about to read a love note by her crush. I unfold the letter and freeze.

You can't run from me, Princess. You're mine. You've always been mine.

I reach for my gun hidden underneath my dress. I pull it out and aim around the room, looking for a place an intruder could be hiding. I look under the bed, the closet, the bathroom, but I'm alone.

My heart is beating wildly. Not because of Beckett anymore, but because there was a true monster in this room.

Adrian and Georgio are right outside. I could tell them

about it, show them the letter. They could pull up the security feed to see who entered my room and how they got in.

But I don't trust them.

I stare at the note. It must have been from the man who was chasing me on Beckett's wedding day.

Shivers break out all over my body. I'm still gripping my gun in one hand and the letter in the other.

I slink to the floor right where I'm standing against a wall opposite my bed as I stare at the letter.

Suddenly, I remember the man who was chasing me.

I've known him my entire life.

He's always wanted me.

Chased me.

Told me I was his.

He's never hurt me, but I've seen him hurt others. I did love before, and he killed them. He's killed everyone I love.

Vincent can't protect me from him.

But maybe Beckett and the Retribution Kings can.

My discarded earrings are on the floor. They were the easiest way to communicate with them, but I destroyed them so they wouldn't know what I gave up for them.

I walk over to my dresser where I keep my burner phones and consider my next options. *Do I contact them or not?*

I type out a quick text to Lucy, letting her know I'm okay.

She responds that she is owed all the dirty details of my sexcapades with Beckett.

I smile.

· · ·

Me: It was like a lightning strike—both exhilarating and painful. But I know you aren't going to accept that as an explanation. The crass version is his dick is huge, and he knows how to use it. I had two orgasms. I was putty in his hands. He ruined me for all other guys.

Lucy: LOL <3 When will I see your pretty face again?

Me: Soon. Hugs.

Lucy: Hugzzzz

I smile, but the truth is I don't know when I'll see her again. I could die tomorrow during the game. That would be the best outcome. The games would have to stop. Beckett and Caius would be safe. Lucy would be safe. And I wouldn't marry a monster.

But I wouldn't have Beckett. I wouldn't have a chance of having him forever. The chance of us both surviving and ending up together is 0.00001%. But still, I'll take those odds.

I stare at my phone, wanting to call him, to hear his voice. But it's dangerous. This phone is hard for Vincent to track, but I have no doubt my room is bugged and Adrian or Georgio are outside my door listening.

But I have to let them know that I'm okay and that I need them to look at the security camera to see if they saw anyone sneak into my room.

I type in the number Gage had me memorize, and then I text like I'm texting an old friend.

I'd love to have coffee with you tomorrow. Unfortunately, I'll have to take a raincheck. My phone has been acting weird, so sorry if I miss your messages. Hugs!

We agreed ahead of time on a few codewords. Hugs mean I'm safe. Kisses mean I need rescuing. Any mention of my phone means I need you to check security cameras.

There is no immediate response, so I don't know if Gage got my message or not.

I distract myself by changing into pajama shorts and a shirt, brushing my teeth, and then climbing into bed with my gun, note, and phone.

I stare at the note for a few more seconds before deciding what to do with it. I climb out of bed and poke my head out into the hallway. "Do either of you have a zippo?"

Georgio has a bag of ice on his face, and he glowers at me. He's useless.

Adrian tosses me one. "Planning on burning the condo down? If so, let me call my wife and tell her goodbye first."

I frown. "You're married? Huh."

"Why would you think I'm not?"

"Just your general demeanor, and you look too young to be married."

"I'm two years older than you. You'll be married by the time you're my age."

Not if I have anything to say about it.

I dart back into my room and burn the letter. The man

who sent it is just trying to scare me. That's who he is. He likes playing games. I won't give him the time of day. I won't let him know he's getting to me. He wins that way. It wouldn't surprise me if he planted a bug in my room, so I'm going to have to be even more careful with what I do or say. But I won't let him scare me.

Gage eventually texts me back: All good! Hugs!

My shoulders slump. *Really? That's all I get?* I'm going crazy over here. But it means he looked at the security cameras and found nothing. It means everyone is safe.

I consider my options. Maybe the monster didn't send the note. Maybe Vincent put it here to spook me, to get me to behave.

It doesn't make sense. I know who sent it—the only man who scares me more than Vincent. Vincent has honor, loyalty, a code he abides by. He kills, but fairly, in a way that men fear but realize is necessary.

Kek—he kills for sport, for fun, because he can. Kek has no men, no wealth, no family to support. He kills. He tortures. He takes what he wants.

He's taken me before. I escaped, but just barely.

He won't make the same mistake if he succeeds in kidnapping me again.

I shiver at what happened last time, at what could happen next.

I fucked up. I've gone so long without loving anyone but Lucy. Vincent protects Lucy. He won't protect Beckett or any of the guys I care about.

It's up to me to protect them.

I can't let him know I care. I can't let him know I love Beckett.

I truly have to give him up and make him hate me.

That should be easy enough. He hated me before; he can hate me again.

But it's going to wreck me.

I close my eyes, hoping the darkness will take me and that Kek won't visit me in my sleep.

But sleep never comes. I'm reliving the memories with Kek. *How did I forget him?* Out of survival. I needed to forget him so I wouldn't spend every second petrified. I would have never gone near Beckett if I had remembered.

I tread out of my bedroom. Adrian must have drawn the short straw because he's the one on guard outside of my bedroom.

I toss his zippo back to him. He doesn't ask what I'm doing up as I head downstairs to the library; he just follows.

I walk along the shelves of books—mostly classics—until I stop on the spine of a book I used to read as a kid. It's a fantasy romance about a princess who lived in a tower. She was cursed until a prince came and saved her.

I take the book off the shelf and curl up with it on the small couch. Taking my gun out, I set it beside me just in case.

Adrian eyes it. "Is there something I should be aware of?"

"Nope, I'll kill the bad guys if they come. Don't worry." I open the first page of my book.

Adrian sighs and sits down on the floor in front of the couch, resting his head back. "I know you will, and that's what scares me."

"Why does it scare you?"

"You shouldn't be able to protect us; it's against the rules. You put on a big display at the first round of games. Some say you just got lucky because none of the guys could fight back. But if they see you fight for real, they'll know. And they can't know."

"Why?"

"They just can't. It's not safe. You can't be a fighter and a princess."

I frown.

I start reading the words in the book about the beautiful princess. How pretty, kind, and gentle she is. How caring of others she is. Never how strong. Never courageous. Never wielding a weapon as well as the prince.

This is what I should be. This is what the mafia demands of their princesses—docile, gorgeous, and weak.

It's not who I am, though. Beckett knew that from the first time he saw me. He called me princess in a mocking voice because he knew I couldn't be farther from the truth.

I'm not a princess. I'm a fighter, a warrior. And a fighter saves herself, as well as her true love, even if it kills her.

2

——————

BECKETT

I'VE PLAYED the video at least a thousand times in the last twenty minutes. I know it's not actually possible, but I did. I've replayed it so many times that I can see every detail when I close my eyes.

I see Ri—no, Rialta—pick the lock of the hotel room door with a small tool. The creak of the door as it opens will haunt me even in my sleep.

Why did I leave Odette? If I was there, she would have been safe.

I watch her walk inside the room in her black leggings and black hoodie pulled up over her head. Even with the hoodie on, I know it's Rialta Corsi. I'd know that ass anywhere.

Odette's eyes get so big with shock they look like they're about to pop out of their sockets as Rialta speaks to her. There are no weapons initially. Eventually, Rialta pulls out a knife from the side of her thigh.

Odette makes it a foot off the bed before Rialta makes her first slice. It's through her forearm—the result of a

15

defensive block that Odette tries to throw up. It's no match for Rialta's skills, though.

Odette stands defenseless until she finally drops to the floor, defeated. Rialta takes some rope casually from the pocket of her hoodie. She ties Odette's wrists together, not that Odette is in any condition to fight back. And then Rialta does the same to her ankles.

The next part is the worst. The piece of tape Rialta puts over Odette's mouth takes away the last thing that could have saved her.

It's only then does Rialta turn. Her profile is in clear view of the camera. I see it all—her raven hair, dark eyes, thick brows and eyelashes, and fierce warrior gleam.

Rialta Corsi is the reason Odette bled. The reason she was kidnapped. The reason she died.

And I have no idea why.

What did Odette ever do to Rialta?

And how did I let myself fall for her for even a second? How could I have fucked the devil, the woman who ruined my entire life?

If it wasn't for her, I would have lived happily with Odette. I would have eventually found out the truth. And then we would have broken up, or we would have fallen in love. Either way, our lives wouldn't have been destroyed. We would have had a chance to figure it out—together.

Now, I'm left to pick up the pieces. There is nothing left but retribution.

Why didn't I teach Odette how to defend herself? Why didn't Caius? Her father? Why—why didn't we teach her like Corsi did his own daughter? If we did, then it would have been a fair fight instead of a slaughter.

I'm sorry about Odette's death. I'm sorry to find out the truth—to find out what could have been. But all I can think about is Ri. No, Rialta. She's not Ri; she's not Princess; she's not my Fighter. She's Rialta Corsi—a lethal assassin working with Corsi. She was playing me this entire time, manipulating me to get me on her side so I would divulge secrets about the Retribution Kings.

How did I not realize it was her sooner? I ran into Rialta in the lobby after that—covered in blood. *How did I not piece it together?*

I didn't want to believe it; I didn't want it to be true. I couldn't imagine the scared, beautiful princess being a killer.

I know what has to happen next, what I have to do about my Rialta problem, but I'm not ready. Sure, the wrath of every storm that has ever rocked this earth lives inside me now. It swirls around in competing circles, threatening to explode out of me and destroy everything in my path. I'm going to spend the rest of my life trying to keep my fury in check.

There is only one solution—kill Rialta for what she did and destroy her father.

But as pissed as I am, I'm not ready to kill her, not yet.

There's a light tap against the door.

"Come in," I say, pulling the flash drive from the computer as I do.

It's Gage—not surprising since I'm using his laptop.

"We got a message from Ri. She's safe but worried about something. She wants me to check the security cameras in their condo."

I nod and hand him the computer. I don't think he notices the change in me, the way my jaw ticks when he calls her Ri instead of a monster. I'm not sure I'm ready to tell them—any of them—the truth. I want to be the one to decide how we handle Rialta. I deserve to be the one.

Rialta.

Rialta.

Rialta.

No matter how many times I say her name, it doesn't feel right. It never will—none of this will.

Gage sinks onto the bed next to me. He pulls up the feeds but doesn't see anything suspicious. Then it's her—Ri, heading up the stairs. I can't hear what her guard behind her says, but it earns him a broken nose.

Gage chuckles at her action.

I glare, unable to unglue my eyes from her, from this woman who is more dangerous than any man in this house, a woman who manipulated us all.

"Do you want to send a message to her?" Gage asks as he types his own message to her.

I think for a moment. I want to let her know that I know. That I'm coming for her. That I'm done playing hero. She doesn't need or want me to anyway, but she's going to need a hero when I'm done with her.

"No," I shake my head.

Gage frowns as he finishes his message to her and hits send. Then he looks at me. I don't know what he sees, but I wish I had Caius's skill of going into the void and showing nothing to the rest of us.

"Who was it? Who killed her?" he asks, his voice calm as he stares at the flash drive.

I should tell him. It's too big of a secret to keep to myself. Everyone's feelings are complicated when it comes to Rialta Corsi.

Just tell him.

Tell him.

My mouth doesn't open; my lips don't even so much as mouth the words. I look down at the flash drive.

Just hand it to him.

He can watch it. That will be the easiest way to explain everything that happened.

My hand clutching the flash drive doesn't budge.

I can't tell him. I can't tell any of them. Not yet. Not until I figure out what I plan on doing to her.

But I have to tell him something. He's not going to just let this go; none of them are.

"There was nothing on it but static. Nothing but Corsi playing with us again," I say.

Gage's eyebrows jump. "Let me take a look at it. Maybe I can salvage some of the footage. It might be encrypted or—"

"No. Your skills are better than mine, but I'm not clueless when it comes to these things. I know what I'm looking at and how to recover lost files. Albeit, I might do it slower than you would."

His head falls back against the headboard. "There's really nothing on it? We got nothing?"

I nod, still gripping the flash drive.

"It was all for nothing?" Caius says from the hallway.

I look him in the eye. I hate lying. I'm not very good at it, and I think it's the lowest of sins you can commit against someone you care about.

But I'm not sure how he'd react if I told him the truth. Plus, he hid the truth from me since I first met him. Not that it makes this better, but I don't want anyone going rogue and either killing Rialta or trying to save her until I figure out a plan for her.

I nod. It seems more like a lie by omission than a straight-out lie.

Caius falls against the door, his face white as his fist

grips the front of his shirt over his chest. It's the most emotion I've seen out of him in a while.

"I shouldn't have left Ri," he says, quietly.

I agree, he shouldn't have. If he'd brought her back, I could have killed her, gotten retribution for Odette, and been done with all of them. I could have left and started over.

My heart skips a beat, not in the I'm head over heels in love sort of way, but in the I have too strong feelings for a girl who killed my wife way.

"Thank you," I finally say, knowing it needs to be said. I can hate Caius all I want. He reminds me too much of Odette. He lied to me. He's kissed Ri countless times just to piss me off. He's fucked her. But he saved my life.

"You would have done the same for me," he says, staring at the blank wall in the bedroom.

I wouldn't have, not for him, but I don't say that.

"The games start tomorrow at nine PM. What are we going to do until then?" Gage asks.

"Sleep. And keep searching for the person who killed Odette," I say.

The guys nod.

"You can sleep in here. This place actually has enough bedrooms for everyone," Caius says.

And then they leave. I wait until the door shuts before I break the flash drive, destroying any evidence that Rialta was the killer. It's stupid of me. The guys will never believe me unless they see her hurting Odette with their own eyes.

I'm not ready to face the truth yet. I'm not ready to just flat-out kill Rialta. I need to play with her first like she did me. Then, I'll kill her.

Yep, she's dead.

My heart clenches, already feeling the pain of losing Ri—she's no more. She never existed in the first place. Apparently, I fall for the fantasy instead of reality.

I fell for Odette, thinking she loved me back, when actually she was just finding a candidate for her family's criminal organization. Nothing about our relationship was real.

I fell for Ri, thinking she was innocent, when in reality she is guiltier than all of us. She will pay the ultimate price for her sins.

Thump, thump—shut up, heart. She deserves to die. I'll deal with you later for falling in love with all the wrong women. You're cut off. You don't get to make my decisions anymore. All you do is cause us pain.

3

RI

ADRIAN PULLS the SUV up to a wooded area near the lake. As he stops the car, I get goosebumps and not the good kind. They scream at me to run the other fucking way. There is danger in these woods.

"Good thing we went to your apartment to get you leggings and tennis shoes, Princess. Although, I'd love to see you hike through the woods in those heels and tight dresses you wear," Georgio smirks.

"Do I need to break your nose again?"

"Do it, and I'll break yours right back. I talked to the boss. He said if you do that again, I should punch back."

My eyes scan through the darkness outside, already done with this conversation. I'm anxious to see what awaits me and whether or not Beckett is already here. I don't have the eerie tingling along my skin like I normally do when I'm near him. I don't have that tug against my heartstrings, begging me to go to him, so he must not be here.

"Did Vincent also tell you if you touch me, you're dead?"

"He told me he wouldn't kill me."

"No, but I will."

Adrian laughs.

Georgio goes white.

I throw the door open, unfazed by my idiot guards. When I put my feet down, I'm thankful that I did convince them to get me some proper clothes for a competition. As much as the kissing game played to my advantage, I doubt every game will. The guys will get better at picking games.

I'm wearing tennis shoes, three-quarter leggings, a tank top, and a black hoodie over it. Right now, I'm thankful for the hoodie; it's keeping me warm.

I walk along a trail through the trees, headed toward voices. The sun set a while ago, so I can barely make out where I'm walking. I pull out my phone to light the path as I hear Adrian and Georgio mumbling behind me.

"No one told me it's fucking cold after dark," Georgio says.

There's a smack.

Adrian smacked him.

I smirk—*good*.

The trail leads to a clearing with a small fire in the middle. Surrounded by the fire's light, I flick off my phone and put it back in my pocket before walking toward the contestants with purpose.

Everyone is dressed for the darkness, wearing black clothes they can easily move in. It seems that everyone got the message that this time will be different than the last game where formal attire was required.

I don't know if the guys realize it's me under this hoodie or not, but they keep chatting with each other, ignoring me. It gives me time to scan for Beckett and Caius, but I don't find either of them.

However, I do find Vincent.

"Boss wants to chat with you," Georgio says.

I sigh and walk over to where he's standing just beyond the crowd surrounding the fire.

"What's wrong? Was I supposed to wear a dress and heels in the middle of the woods?" I ask, sarcastically.

"If you'd stay out of the games, then yes. You were supposed to look like the beautiful princess, a prize to be won. You would have been safe. But no, you had to throw your name in. Now, not even I can ensure your safety."

I cross my arms, annoyed with him. "I can ensure my own safety just fine, thank you."

He sighs, like he can't believe I'm his daughter, and this is what he has to put up with. He looks like he's aged overnight. I don't know what has him so troubled, but something happened, something changed.

"I chose the name yesterday. I figured it would give the men time to think of an appropriate game and for us to do with any setup. I didn't want a repeat of last time," he says.

I nod, "Makes sense."

"This game is dangerous."

"I'm sure I can handle myself."

"You could—but I'm calling in my debt. You owe me. You promised to do what I ask, when I ask it. Let's see if you were lying more or not."

I hold my breath, waiting to see what horrible thing I'm going to have to do. It will be worth it. Caius lives. Beckett lives. Saving them is worth any cost.

"You're going to lose, badly. You are going to act like you've never seen a gun, let alone shot one. Do you understand me?"

I nod, slowly. I hate this. It means I can't defend myself.

It means he wants me to play a damsel in distress. It means he wants me to hide my skills.

"Lose, let them shoot you, but don't die. Think you can handle that?"

My eyes wide. *Let them shoot me? Don't die?* Shit, I don't know what this game is, but it doesn't sound like what he's asking is going to be easy.

"If you don't, I'll kill him," he looks behind me. I turn my head to where Caius and Beckett are standing near the fire. They're both dressed in all black. Caius says something to Beckett, but Beckett just stands sternly, focused, his brows furrowed, deep in thought.

I don't know which *him* Vincent is talking about—Caius or Beckett. I don't know if he's figured out that Beckett is whom I really care about. He's whom I'd do anything for. Caius, I'd just do most things for.

"I'll do it," I say.

"Don't fail. If you die, everything we've worked for is ruined."

We've worked for.

I sigh. I don't know what he means or why he thinks we are on the same side, but we most definitely are not.

I walk back toward the fire with my two shadows behind me. I doubt they will be close, keeping me safe during this game.

Vincent approaches the group, and everyone turns to him as he speaks, "Welcome. This is the second game and is far more deadly than the first. Thank you all for coming. I'm excited to see who has what it takes to marry Rialta."

He points, and all eyes burn into me. Lust attacks me from all sides.

I'm no longer forbidden.

I don't know if these guys know that yet, but I'm going to hate finding out.

"I drew a name yesterday—Leighton Stone. Would you please do the honors of explaining the game you've chosen?"

A man steps forward from the darkness and into the light of the fire next to Vincent. The man is tall, with an endless amount of muscles, short reddish-brown hair, and a look of danger that oozes from his pores.

"The game is easy—it's like laser tag or paintball, except with real guns. You get shot, you're out. When you lose, you find your way back home and get your own medical care. That is, if you can survive that long. The last man standing wins Rialta for the week."

Wins me.

I hate this. My insides churn at the thought. Last time I could fight back even though I knew I wasn't going to win. This is a game I actually have a shot at winning, but I can't fight. I can't shoot. I have to lose and hope whoever shoots me only shoots me in the arm or leg and misses every major artery.

And Beckett could be shot. He could die.

That's my new mission: ensure he survives. I can't shoot. I can't protect myself. I can't show my skills, but I can ensure that he stays alive.

"The only rules are you must stay within a mile of this fire, and the only weapon you can use is a gun. Break either of those rules and you're disqualified. Does anyone need a weapon, or did everyone bring at least a gun?" Leighton continues.

The crowd chuckles.

"Rialta will need a gun," Vincent says.

I sigh. I already have one shoved in the back of my

leggings, but it's hidden by my sweatshirt. Clearly, Vincent wants everyone to think I've never touched a gun before in my life.

Georgio hands me a gun. "Aim with this end, squeeze with this; it's called a trigger. And mind the recoil." He snickers. He knows I know how to use a gun.

"Thanks for your excellent instruction." I fake not knowing how to load bullets, and Georgio pretends to show me how.

Despite the terrible acting, the guys closest seem to be fooled by the ruse. I glance over at Vincent, who looks to be smiling with approval. *Am I dead?* Because his approval is not possible.

He then steps forward, back into the full light of the fire, his smile long gone. "On the count of three." He gives us no other warning.

I try to consider my options, what I should do. This is about to be a massacre. Vincent wants me to lose, but he also said not to die. If I stay here, I'll die. The shots will be too close range. Even if they guys try not to kill me, a stray bullet will take me out easily enough.

"One."

Everyone readies their guns.

"Two."

The air changes, from cool to hot in an instant.

"Three."

I run.

Others do as well.

The ring of gunfire behind me tells me many did not. Several stayed and were shot.

I run as fast as I can into the woods, darting between two trees. There isn't really a trail, just rough underbrush that immediately scratches me as I dive to the ground as gunfire whizzes past my head.

Really? Vincent spent years ensuring my safety, hired bodyguards and the best security systems to protect me every moment of every day. All of that only to let me die like this. Unbelievable.

I toss aside the gun Georgio gave me. I have a second one anyway. And since I'm not supposed to use it, it's just dead weight.

I do a pushup and hop back onto my feet to keep running. I can't run forever. Eventually, someone will shoot me. I'll have to let someone shoot me.

I need to find the right guy to shoot me. One who will make it as painless as possible. I need to find Beckett or Caius. They won't like it, but they'll do it.

Or could I shoot myself?

I decide I'll do it if it's my only option, but it's far less painful if someone else shoots me. So I keep running, until I no longer hear the crunch of footsteps behind me.

I stop, leaning against a tree as blood oozes down my arms and legs from all the scrapes of thorns, sticks, and trees. I breathe in and out, trying to catch my breath before I have to run again.

I look behind me. I can see the firelight in the distance, so I didn't run that far. I hear the whoosh of water hitting a shoreline behind me. I'm close to a lake.

I scan the woods. A shadow moves behind a tree about twenty feet from me.

I freeze.

I don't know if he sees me. I don't know who it is. I don't know if I should run or stay still.

I continue to still, holding my breath and hoping he doesn't see me—at least, not until I figure out who he is.

"I think you dropped your gun, Princess. It'll be hard to win without one," Leighton says, walking out from behind the tree.

Shit, now what do I do?

Will he actually shoot me? Do I run? Do I pull my gun on him?

I can't.

Vincent will kill Caius or Beckett or Lucy if I do.

I close my eyes, deciding not to run. If I run, it'll make me a harder target. If Leighton shoots me, I want him to have a clear shot.

Any guy who shoots me should know better than to make it fatal. I just have to hold still enough for him to shoot me in the arm, the leg, or just graze the skin if he knows what he's doing. I have no idea how good of a shot Leighton is, but I suspect pretty good if he came up with this idea.

I hold my breath, my eyes piercing his as I watch him aim his gun in my direction.

"Don't worry. I'll make this painless, Princess. And then when I win you, I'll show you how it feels to be protected by me."

"I doubt you're a good enough shot to leave me devoid of pain or scars."

He smirks. "You have no idea."

"Do your worst," I say.

And then I feel the bullet.

It's not a graze; it's a sledgehammer rammed through my arm.

I look down at my right bicep, where a bullet is now lodged.

"Rialta! Are you okay?" Leighton yells as he runs toward me.

He wasn't the one who shot me.

I look behind me and see dark eyes staring at me.

I frown because I know those eyes. They don't belong to a monster. They belong to my friend, my lover, the man I'm in love with.

He stares at me for one long second. I don't see any remorse, regret, or confusion about whom he was shooting.

Beckett meant to shoot me, and he didn't just graze my arm.

But why?

I never get the chance to ask him. He disappears into the darkness just as Leighton approaches, fawning over me like I have a fatal wound.

Why?

4

BECKETT

"THREE," Corsi says, and chaos erupts.

Men start shooting like we're in the middle of a battle-field and everyone is the enemy. The smart ones take off toward the woods, toward cover.

I scan across the fire and see Ri running into the woods.

Wise.

But it pisses me off. I want to watch her fight and get shot.

Except, she's one of the best fighters. She won't get shot, not without a fight. Knowing her, she's about to climb a tree and rain down bullets on all of us. I don't know what that little act was before, pretending she'd never held a gun before, but I'm curious to find out.

I run along the edge of the forest, careful to avoid stray bullets as I follow Ri into the forest.

She's fast and has a head start on me, even though the thick brush is a pain in the ass to run through. But I stay no more than thirty feet behind her—my gun tingling for me to use it in my hand.

Seeing a shadow on my left, I only look long enough to ensure it isn't Caius before shooting him in the gut. The man falls with a loud groan.

I won't shoot to kill, but I'm not going to make it easy for any of the men to survive their wounds either.

What are you going to do when you catch Ri?

I don't know.

Am I following her to keep her safe? My heart aches so fucking bad thinking about her. About what could have been. About how fooled I was.

Do I want to shoot her, kill her? This would be the perfect place. No one would see that I was the one who shot her. It would be clean and tidy, even if it would ignite an all-out war over Corsi's power.

Ri falls to the ground as a bullet whizzes past, and my breath is knocked out of me.

No!

But a second later, she's back on her feet, and I let out a sigh of relief. Apparently, I'm not ready for her to die yet, or I want to be the one to pull the trigger.

I run after her but notice one large difference. She no longer has a gun.

Why?

In fact, I didn't see her fire it once. That's not the fighter I know.

She stops suddenly, leaning against a tree, trying to catch her breath, and probably beating herself up for dropping her gun.

I circle around her until I'm at her back, watching her.

Leighton approaches and talks to her. He raises his gun, but I'm faster.

I don't think—I just shoot.

My bullet hits her hard in her right bicep. I don't know

if Leighton was only going to graze her skin with his bullet. I don't know if I did her a favor or hurt her worse than she deserved.

My heart trembles in my chest. My eyes glaze as she looks at me. A tornado of emotions howls through me—glee, fear, lust, terror, vengeance.

I turn and run before Ri has a chance to call me out and before I do something stupid like carry her out of here.

I hate her.

I want her.

I everything but love her.

"Why the hell did you shoot her like that?" Caius says from my left.

I stumble to a stop.

I don't know—*maybe because she's responsible for Odette's death?* She stabbed her. She may have later shot her.

But I don't tell Caius that.

Instead, I hold my hand above my head as my chest tightens. It must be because I'm out of breath, not because my heart hurts.

"You could have just grazed her. You didn't have to actually shoot her in the arm. That recovery is going to take forever and she's right-handed." He stares at my missing right arm. "You of all people should know not to shoot your friend in their dominant arm."

She's not my friend. She's my enemy.

I raise my gun, about to aim at Caius, but he beats me to it.

I feel the burn of the bullet as it brushes against my outer thigh, doing more damage to my jeans than to my skin. But I see a couple of drops of blood as Caius runs back toward Ri.

I wish the wound would have hit deeper. Maybe then I would be too consumed with the pain to register any other feeling—not that I understand how I'm feeling exactly.

Every step I take back toward the campfire is agony. Every stride feels like a step away from Ri.

You shot her, you asshole. You're the last person she would want to see.

She's safe with Leighton and Caius. They won't let her get shot more. And I just shot her in the arm. It's nowhere near fatal, even if it is painful.

I think back to losing my arm and shudder.

I'm a monster, but she deserved it.

She deserves a fate far worse.

I take my time making it back to the campfire, careful not to accidentally run into someone's loose bullet. Eventually, I make it back into the light glow of the fire.

The fire doesn't provide much light, but it's enough to see at least a dozen dead bodies lying in the dirt. No one has tried to move them yet. Corsi is sitting on a log drinking a whiskey with his guards like he isn't feet away from decomposing corpses.

I know he's ruthless, but this feels low, even for him. It's one of the reasons I never wanted to be a leader. I don't ever want to become this callous about taking lives. I never want to be feared so much that I don't even respect human life.

I continue around the circle, to the side that seems to have mostly alive men. Some seem to just have grazes or nicks, flesh wounds that will heal easily enough. Others are moaning in pain. If they have any allies, they are getting tended to or helped to the cars. If they don't, then they'll eventually join those who've already died.

I spot Caius, sitting on the ground, leaning against a tree trunk as he holds his shoulder tightly. And then I see the blood.

Fuck.

I run to him, removing my shirt and tying it around the wound to form a tourniquet.

"We need to get you out of here. You need that cleaned and stitched, and you might need a blood transfusion."

Caius looks at his wound. "In just a second, I think Corsi is about to announce the winner."

I frown but hold my hand against the wound and the bleeding comes to a stop. I assess the amount of blood on his shirt and the color of the blood on his skin—still pink. He's got some time before he bleeds to death.

I want to know who won as well.

"By the way, I didn't realize it was Ri I shot. My eyesight is shit in the dark. I was in shock when you approached me. I couldn't believe I shot her."

"Noted—you can't see in the dark. But I don't think Ri will forgive you that easily for shooting her," Caius smirks, thinking he's going to get her to kiss him or even fuck him again before she forgives me. That is until I tell him the truth.

Corsi stands. "It appears we have a winner—Leighton Stone."

People grumble; some applaud.

Corsi looks to his left, where I assume Leighton is sitting. I don't know why he doesn't stand. *Is he wounded too? Just the last to get shot?*

"Congrats. Your prize is you get Rialta for the week. She's no longer forbidden from sex. You can do with her as you please."

Everyone falls silent as he says she's no longer forbidden. My breath catches, my heart slams to a stop, and my skin prickles with fear.

No longer forbidden—*Ri, what did you do to save us? And why would you when you killed Odette? Did you really want me that badly that you'd kill my wife? Did you really think I'd love you after what you did?*

"The only rule is that you keep her safe. You keep her alive, which by the looks of her at the moment, is going to be hard. If she dies, I'll hold you and everyone you care about responsible, Leighton," Corsi says with a growl so fierce I don't know how I'm going to get that sound out of my head.

Does Corsi really care about his daughter? Or just her survival so he can find a man to marry into his family?

I don't know why he's so worried. I just shot her in the arm. She's fine.

But then Leighton stands to leave, and I see why he wasn't standing before. Ri is in his arms, completely limp. Blood falls like a river down her body from her arm, even though he has his shirt wrapped around it.

"I'll take good care of her, sir," Leighton says, and then he starts jogging.

I start walking after her.

"You can't," Caius says.

"I..." I'm speechless. I just shot her in the arm...she can't be dying. I don't understand what happened.

"You must have hit an artery," Caius says.

I hit an artery.

Me.

If she dies, it's my fault as much as Leighton's. I'm not letting him off the hook. He came up with this game.

I need to go after her. I need to see that she survives.

Only so you can kill her all over again, the darkness within me says.

Only so you can have a chance to forgive her, the light says.

But the guilt—damn, is it strong.

"Help me up, and stitch me up on the way. We can follow and make sure she's okay," Caius says.

I put my arm under his shoulder and help him up. We walk together back to the car—the secret threatening to spill out of me with every step.

I can't tell him. He'd hate her. He'd want to follow in order to ensure she's dead, not to save her.

As much as I know that's the right thing to do, what should be done, I'm not ready for her to die yet. I'm not done messing with her, ruining her life. I'm not done fucking her yet.

5

RI

Beckett shot me.

Why?

Beckett shot me.

Why?

It was a mistake?

He was saving me?

He hates me?

He knows what you really are—a monster?

"Wake up, Beautiful," a calming male voice says.

Pain ricochets through my body. My arm feels numb. The blood my heart is forcing through my body is sandpaper in my veins. It feels too dry, too little. I need more blood to survive.

"I need you to stay with me, Princess. I can save you, but only if you stay with me. Promise you'll stay with me, or your father is going to kill me, and then we'll both be dead. I'd much rather spend my time with you here than in hell."

A hero came to save me. But not my hero. No, my hero shot me. He's the reason I'm bleeding out, about to die.

Why?

Why?

WHY?

"Stay with me so you can show me how good your shooting skills really are. I didn't fall for that 'I've never touched a gun' act. I know you can shoot. I know you can fight, show me how much of a fighter you are."

Fighter.

That's what Beckett used to call me. It was his nickname. So *why is this stranger calling me it?*

Fighter, you have to fight.

So I do.

I fight.

I open my eyes, and his hazel ones stare down at me. He flashes me a crooked grin.

"Hello, Beautiful. You're going to be okay," Leighton says, stroking my hair. Someone else is driving.

"Where are we going?"

"To the hospital."

I frown. "You can't take me to the hospital. They will ask too many questions."

His smile brightens. "Not when you're me. Your father isn't the only one with pull in the city. I could take you back to my place, and you'd survive, but I thought we'd get you a full checkup. I don't want you dying on me; I'm far too young to die."

I smile lightly. He is young, maybe a year or two older than me. Unlike Beckett, who is almost a decade my elder.

I thought I'd like a guy close to my age, but Beckett pulls at my heartstrings like no other man.

Although, this man may be sweeter than I thought he'd be. Funnier too. He reminds me of Hayes. The world hasn't hardened him yet, which is surprising given his surroundings.

The car stops.

"I'm going to lift you out. Don't pass out on me. Talk to me, tell me something no one else knows," Leighton says.

I think for a moment. I shouldn't say anything. But I blame it on the blood loss. "If Vincent hadn't made me lose, I'd have won. I'd even have beaten you, Saint."

He laughs, his eyes turning devious. "I imagine you would. Which is why you have to live long enough so I can see it for myself." He leans in closer. "And by the way, I'm no saint, but I do love that you gave me a nickname."

And then I'm on a gurney. Finally, I close my eyes and shut everything out.

My eyes flicker open. The room is dark, except for an annoyingly bright light over my bed burning my retinas.

I immediately shut my eyes again, waiting until the feeling goes away. I squint my eyes open again, looking away from the light.

I'm in a hospital room. There's an IV in my left arm, and my right is heavily bandaged in a sling. I can't feel either. I glance at the IV pole. They must be pumping me full of morphine.

I sigh, my head is already fuzzy from the drugs. I know morphine is different than heroin or whatever drugs I was filled with before, but my body reacts the same way to it. I don't want to be on painkillers. I don't want to chance losing my memories again.

I look for a call button to get a nurse to remove the IV. I can't move my right arm, and I don't see any button within reach of my left hand. In fact, I don't see a call button at all.

"Looking for this?" a voice says from the shadows, holding a beige device with a call button on it.

The voice hits me in the chest—*Beckett.*

It can't be, though. He didn't win. Leighton did. This can't be real. I'm either imagining him or hallucinating his voice over Leighton's.

I stare at the shadow, hoping it will reveal itself. The man steps forward, just enough that he's no longer a black bob. Dark jeans wrapped around thick muscles, a dark shirt where a veiny forearm protrudes. I don't have to keep traveling up to know what I'm going to find. A sharp jawline, a devilish smirk, and dark eyes that can only belong to one person—*Beckett.*

"Expecting someone else?" he asks with a smug expression.

"It's really you, Hero?" I croak, my voice dry.

He frowns, the lines in his face tighten. "You're not hallucinating me."

"How are you here?" I look around. "Where is Leighton?"

"The good thing about Leighton being the leader is he doesn't have time to sit around all night and wait for you to wake up. He had business he had to attend to. His guards were easy enough to slip by."

I raise an eyebrow. "You're a leader too. Doesn't that mean that you have responsibilities away from here?"

"No," he says simply. His voice is deep and commanding. Then his gaze drifts to my arm. His furrow deepens, and he reaches for his own right arm, his missing arm. He grabs for it absentmindedly while staring at my arm.

When he comes up empty, grabbing air instead of his arm, he looks down, remembering his own loss.

He squeezes his eyes shut as the agony overtakes him like a wave crashing down on top of him. From where I lay, watching him, it looks like he's drowning, fighting for air and not getting any, no matter how hard he kicks for the surface.

"You okay?" I ask.

"Me? I should be asking you that," he says through his own pain.

"You must have gotten shot, too. Otherwise, you would have won."

He lifts his leg, and I see the small flesh wound on his outer thigh.

I open my mouth to ask him why he shot me, but instead, I ask, "How did you lose your arm?"

He stares at me like I just asked him a complicated math question. He won't tell me. It was rude of me to ask anyway. I shouldn't intrude.

But then he exhales a long breath. "An explosion."

My eyebrows raise as his eyes glaze over with overwhelming memories. His entire body tightens, veins bulge in his forearm, neck, and forehead, and his muscles convulse.

I shouldn't have asked. I didn't mean to cause him pain.

"I was with my brother and the woman who eventually became his wife. We were running down a dock. The explosion happened just as we made it to the end. It flung us into the water."

His chest rises and falls, and I want to jump from the bed to go hug him. The IV, drugs, and injured arm keep me in bed. I'm not sure he'd appreciate my embrace anyway.

"The water was cold. Even after we got out of the water, I still felt cold. That's when I knew." He closes his eyes as his nightmare replays in his head. "Enzo and Kai tried to do everything they could to save my arm, but there was nothing left to do, but…"

My eyes open wide, and my heart aches for this man. "Tell me you didn't endure that pain. Tell me you were unconscious when they…" I can't say it either.

"Sawed my arm off."

I wince as his pain whips in me like cold lightning through my body.

"I was awake for more than I want to remember."

A tear springs from the corner of my eye, burning down my cheek. I wish I could take his suffering away even now. It's a trauma he'll never forget, one that has influenced every aspect of his life.

"But that wasn't the worst part. Sure it hurt like hell, but it only lasted a few minutes." He sucks in a breath, and his chest heaves. His eyes lock on mine. "The worst part was the next day, when I woke up without a part of myself. When I realized that everything changed. I would always be looked at with pity in others' eyes. I would struggle to relearn how to do everything I once took for granted. I would never be whole again. Others would always look at me as deformed, as less than, as incapable of the same things others do."

My tears are falling freely now. He's lost so much. He lost a part of him. He lost the love of his life in Odette. And there is nothing I can do to give him back what he's lost.

A wicked grin spreads across his face. "Don't worry,

Princess, you won't lose your arm. All you need is some physical therapy, and you'll be good as new."

I wipe my tears away with a half-hiccup, half-smile.

He called me Princess, not Fighter.

"I'm not worried if I did," I say, trying my best to let him know I don't see him any differently. What he went through doesn't define him.

He chuckles ominously. "You should be."

The machine to my left whizzes to life. A blood pressure cuff around my arm tightens, checking my blood pressure. It's higher than it should be because I'm so wrapped up in Beckett. He's in pain, so I'm in pain.

Liquid starts pumping from the machine through the line in my IV.

Painkillers.

I feel the warmth as it hits the back of my hand.

I squirm, but I can't get my left hand to bend in such a way to remove the catheter. And I can't move my right arm at all. I try to scrape the IV against the fabric to remove it, but it doesn't budge.

Beckett is at my side in an instant. He gently pulls the tape off before pulling the catheter out of my arm. He reaches behind him and finds gauze to presses against the back of my hand to stop the bleeding.

I should thank him, but the constricting feelings in my chest finally get me to ask the question I should have asked the second I woke up.

"Why?" I rasp, staring at where he's holding my hand like he cares about me. I can't understand his conflicting actions. *Does he care about me or hate me? Is he just using me?*

He doesn't answer right away, and the pull of my curiosity takes hold as I finally meet his eyes. They look as confused and conflicted as I feel.

"It was a mistake. My eyesight is shit in the dark. I thought I was aiming for the outside of your arm, but I missed. I never meant to hit your arm."

I read his face. It's a lie—*all of it.*

My breath quickens as my anger spreads. *Why is he lying to me?*

I need answers.

I pull my hand away, and he lets me.

"I'm so sorry, Ri. When I saw you in Leighton's arms, unconscious, bleeding out—" his words suddenly stop as his nostrils flare and his hand fists, fighting his own feelings.

His words are genuine. These are the truth.

So why did he shoot me? It's not because he can't see well in the dark. I've seen his skills. The darkness wouldn't stop him.

I have to have answers.

I don't have much mobility or strength, but Beckett is close enough that I jab my fingers into his leg wound.

He reacts as I knew he would. He bends over to swat me away, barely acting like I hurt him worse than a bee sting. But I'm not trying to hurt him.

I grab his gun and aim for his heart.

His lopsided grin appears on his face like he finds me adorable, but he knows the truth. I'll use it. I'll kill him if I have to.

"Tell me the truth," I say, my breathing so fast that I'm practically panting.

"You go first." He cocks his head, waiting for me.

Except I have no idea what he's talking about.

"You going to pull that memory loss act on me again?" He leans closer until the gun is stabbing him in the chest. It will probably cause a bruise, but he doesn't seem to care. His eyes scan mine, looking for something, but all he'll find is the fire growing inside me.

A fire flamed with anger. Marked with loss. And encircled with desire.

He leans back after realizing all my emotions. "You won't shoot me."

"Just like you'd never shoot me," I counter. "Oh, wait, except that you did. Your explanation is bullshit, Hero. I've seen you in action. You don't miss. And you can see better than most in the dark. You shot me because you wanted to. Why?"

He's silent for a moment, and I get lost in his dark eyes. Eyes I still love despite him being the one who shot me, being the one who hurt me. There has to be a reason. I'll find out sooner or later, and then I'll judge his actions, decide if he is worthy of my love or not.

Suddenly, he captures my lips with his. I lower the gun, aiming more for his stomach than his chest. His kiss is soft and gentle as his tongue pushes between my lips like he's trying to figure out how much pain I'm in by the taste of my tongue against his.

Once he's reassured that I'm fine, his tongue twists against mine in that familiar battle I'm used to. I let my guard down as he kisses me, pouring his feelings into the kiss. Feelings neither of us understand—but it doesn't feel like he hates me, doesn't feel like he wants me dead. It feels like he's lost without me.

He pulls away and stares at me, unblinking. "Sometimes it's better if we don't know all the answers, Fighter. Sometimes you just have to trust that the person you thought was a monster is really a hero after all."

He stares at my arm like it tortures him. "It won't happen again." He closes his eyes, closing in his pain.

His eyes reopen a moment later. "I owe you a save, Princess. I'll be watching."

I lower my gun as he walks away. "You owe me two saves."

He stops, turning his head.

"I should shoot you, but I'm going to give you the benefit of the doubt. So you owe me twice—once for shooting me and the second to deserve my mercy."

His lips turn up, and he gives the slightest nod before he disappears. I'm left with nothing but the tingle of our kiss on my lips and the strange feeling that I shouldn't have let him off easy. I should have shot him.

6

———

BECKETT

I KISSED her instead of killing her. I'm so fucked.

I've now had two chances to kill her—in the woods and in her hospital room. I passed them both by.

At the very least, I could have questioned her further. I should have tortured her until she admitted the truth.

But all I could think was how could I have shot her? How could I have shot her in the same arm I lost? How could I have risked that loss? How could I have risked her life?

I don't regret often, but I regret shooting her—hurting her. I'm a monster unworthy of happiness, joy, love. I deserve to be miserable. The universe has told me that time and time again. Ri, Odette, before...

I'm a monster, a villain, a creature so tormented, banned from love. I have to stop looking for it. It's the only way to stop hurting everyone around me.

I press the button on the elevator that leads to Caius's apartment in the city. When the doors slide open, I step inside, thankful that no one else is on the elevator. But then I'd be surprised to see anyone here at three in the morning.

My shoulders slump against the wall, and my eyes fall heavy until they finally close. All I can picture is her—Ri. Her peacefully lying asleep in the hospital bed, her hair swept across the pillow, her arm heavily bandaged, and her breathing so slow and steady. I could have watched her sleep for hours, but it was complete torture.

My heart has never beat so fast; my lungs have never worked so hard for breath; my eyes have never slowed so much, afraid that I would miss a single moment. I was terrified that if I closed my eyes, she'd drift away, and it'd all be my fault.

But then the images of her slicing into Odette's flesh flood out the memories of Ri lying broken in the hospital bed.

Why did you have to hurt her, Ri? Did your father threaten to kill you if you didn't? Are you a trained assassin? Were you happy to do your father's bidding? Were you jealous that I married her instead of you?

I can't make sense of Ri's actions. And I can't even start to make sense of my feelings for her. If you had told me that when I found Odette's killer that I would hesitate to get retribution, I would have called you insane.

I should have never stuck my dick in her. That has to be it. I'm confusing my lust with actual feelings for her. I just need a little more time and space. She needs to heal, so I'll stop looking at her like she's a sick puppy.

The elevator doors open, and I step out, trying to shake any lingering emotions.

I run my tongue over my bottom lip without thinking, and my brain turns to our kiss.

That damn kiss.

I shouldn't have kissed her. Her pheromones must be

playing with my mind, making me feel things that aren't there.

Think about how she stole your gun. How she pressed it into your chest. How she threatened to kill you for not telling her why you shot her.

I groan as my cock hardens in my pants just thinking about her holding a gun. Of course, her threatening me turns me on.

I'm so fucked up. She's my villain, and I'm hers. We should hate each other and want to destroy each other, not fuck each other.

I open the door to the apartment. I just want a fair fight; that's why I'll wait for Ri to heal first, then I'll kill her.

Gage is sitting at his computer in the dining room when I walk in. I assume the others are already in bed asleep.

"How is she?" I ask, even though I just left her less than twenty minutes ago.

"Telling the nurses and doctors she's fine and they can release her," Gage says.

I grin at that as I round the table and stare at the computer screen. One of the nurses is trying to convince her to put the IV back in, but Ri is refusing.

Then Leighton comes in and she stares at him warily.

He smiles warmly at her as he approaches her bed. It takes everything inside me not to run back over there, kick his ass, and drag her back here.

Caius joins us, looking like death. His shoulder is stitched up as he walks in only wearing sweatpants, tearing Gage and I's attention from the screen to him.

"My father's dead," Caius says, his eyes wide like he can't believe the words leaving his mouth.

Gage jumps up from the computer and runs to Caius. "You okay?"

Caius nods, but Gage pulls him in for a hug anyway.

Caius doesn't return his hug. He just stands frozen. He's dealt with so much loss lately. I don't know how he hasn't cracked, but he hasn't.

"Lennox, Hayes," Gage yells down the hallways as he releases Caius.

Lennox jogs down the hallway first in just his boxers. He takes one look at the situation then says, "Fuck, I'm sorry."

He hugs Caius quickly before Hayes makes it down the hallway wearing sweatpants.

Lennox walks to him. "Get dressed. Monroe just died."

Hayes runs his hand through his messy long hair. "Jesus, can today get any worse?"

"Yes, it can," I say, because it always can. If I told them about Ri, it would get a lot worse.

They both walk back down the hallway to get dressed, while I finally come to my senses.

"So what happens next?" I ask Gage, not sure that Caius is stable enough to answer. He just lost his father, and he's dealing with a lot of blood loss.

"You have to finish your initiation, so no one else tries to challenge you for leadership," Gage says.

"Don't look at me, I'm done challenging him. You have my full support," Caius says, rubbing his arm and trying to stretch it.

"Do you want someone to take you to the hospital to say goodbye?" I ask Caius.

"No, I knew this was coming. I already said my goodbyes. I want to be at initiation to show my support for you to help with the transition. That's what Dad would have wanted," Caius says.

Lennox returns with a shirt and pants on and a shirt for Caius, which he helps him into.

"So the final part of initiation will happen tomorrow?" I ask.

"No, now. We need to get to the complex ASAP," Caius answers.

"But I thought the initiation wouldn't be final until after I got retribution for Odette?" I ask.

Caius stares straight at me, like he knows something I don't. Like he can see through me. Like he knows the truth that I'm hiding.

"Gage found out who killed Odette," he says.

7

RI

LESS THAN A MINUTE after Beckett leaves, the nurses and doctors start swarming me. Trying to get me to put the IV back in. Telling me I shouldn't get out of bed. Telling me I need to stay here for a few days to ensure I didn't lose too much blood.

But I hate hospitals. It would probably be the safer option to stay here, but my skin is already crawling to get out of here. I need to follow Beckett and figure out what the hell is going on, what he isn't telling me.

The door opens as a nurse fusses over my low blood pressure when Leighton enters.

"Can you give us some privacy?" he asks the nurse.

She smiles at him, releasing my arm. "Of course, Mr. Stone."

Leighton waits for the nurse to leave before he comes over to my side. He takes my hand like we're lovers and then sits on the edge of my bed.

"I'm glad you're awake. Sorry I had to leave. I had a couple of business things to take care of, but I'm completely yours for the rest of the week."

The rest of the week—I hate the sound of that.

I smile tightly. "I'm sure your business needs you more than I need you sitting next to me in this hospital bed every day."

He reaches out, tucking my matted hair behind my ear. "I talked with one of the doctors. You'll be able to leave tonight."

I bite my lip, unsure if I'm happy or scared to death to go home with this man.

Leighton's eyes twinkle with concern as he sits and stares at me like he's madly in love with me.

He's just being sweet. Or he's a psycho.

"Unless you're not ready to leave? I assumed you removing your IV means you want to leave?" he raises his eyebrows, waiting for my answer.

"I'm ready to leave as soon as it's safe."

"Good, I'll arrange it with your doctor. I have my own medical staff that can continue treating you at my house, so it shouldn't be a problem for you to leave."

"Thank you," I say, quietly.

"You gave me quite the scare. There was so much blood loss I thought you might lose your arm."

"I won't, though?"

"No, the doctor was able to repair the damage. But you'll be in that sling for six weeks."

I frown.

He chuckles. "You're adorable when you pout."

"I'm not pouting, I'm frowning."

"Of course, frowning." His smile gets bigger, showing off more of his perfectly straight, white teeth.

"I can understand why you're upset. It's going to be harder to fight in the competition with an injured arm.

But I hope by the end of the week, you'll think I'm a worthy choice and be rooting for me to win."

Now I'm glaring. "I want to choose whom I marry and even if I marry. I don't want a guy to compete for me."

"So feisty, I love it. But you're right. You should be able to choose. That's why I chose the game I did; I'd heard that you were skilled. I was giving you a chance to win. But something happened, didn't it?"

I consider my choices. I could fake innocence, like I don't know what he's talking about. I could come clean or tell him a half-truth.

"Why did you think I was skilled?" I ask, deciding to just avoid answering altogether.

"I saw how you were during the first game. When you kicked my ass, I knew that you had training. I just assumed it carried over to guns as well. Sorry if that was my mistake."

"I appreciate the gesture," I say, still avoiding answering his question. It's clear that Leighton wants me to like him. I decide to see how far I can push him to get what I want. "It's been a long day. Any chance I can recover in my own bed in my own apartment? I'd love to see my roommate and her dog."

He strokes my cheek, and I try not to cringe at his touch. I don't know how I want to play this yet. Maybe I should just kick his ass instead of letting him touch me.

"My place is just as comfortable. Don't worry, I'll make sure you rest easy."

Then, before I realize what he's doing, his lips brush against mine. It's a quick kiss, but not something I asked for nonetheless.

"Ready to blow this joint? I harassed the doctor to let you out early."

I nod.

Twenty minutes later, I'm dressed in some sweats the hospital had on hand and am being wheeled out in a wheelchair to Leighton's car.

He opens the door, and I move to stand, but he grabs my unharmed arm before I fully stand. "Let me help you. You've lost a lot of blood, so you need to take it easy."

The way the world around me is spinning tells me that he's right, but I don't like him putting his hands on me. He helps me up into the SUV before going around and climbing into the backseat next to me.

We start moving almost immediately as a man in the driver's seat pulls us out of the parking lot without speaking to Leighton.

I study Leighton closer, and that's when I finally spot the ghost tattoo as chills race through me. "You're Phantom Brotherhood?"

He nods. "You're looking at the new leader."

My skin crawls, and there is no doubt that he's a monster. Whatever charm he's been giving me is all an act. I should have stayed at the hospital. It would have been safer, even if I was pumped full of drugs and forgot all my memories. It would have been better than getting in this car with him.

I still, trying to think of what I should do next. "You want revenge for Ares's death, don't you? That's what this is about—hurting me to hurt my father."

"No, I'm thankful to your father for killing Ares. I would have never become the leader without him doing that."

He leans in closer to me, and I try to fake a smile. I keep my cool, acting like he doesn't give me the creeps.

The car stops in front of a building, and an eery darkness washes over me. I don't have to look outside to know where we are.

The driver steps out and opens my door, holding his hand out to me. Reluctantly, I take his hand and step out as Leighton runs around the car to help me.

"Are we just making a quick stop here, or do you live here?" I ask, staring at the club. The same club where Caius, Hayes, Lennox, and Gage fucked me. Where Beckett kissed me. Where I watched Vincent kill Ares.

Leighton grins as he takes my uninjured arm, linking our fingers together like we're lovers. "I thought this was the best place for us to enjoy our time together. I'm still moving into a new condo since I've gotten my new title and earnings. But you'll be well taken care of here."

I swallow down the anxiety creeping up my throat as Leighton leads me into the club.

Loud music pounds through my exhausted body. I'm still groggy from the drugs and blood loss, and the sound is doing nothing to help my headache.

Thankfully, Leighton takes me through a door away from the booming music and people. The door closes behind us, and my eyes adjust to my surroundings. It's then that I realize that we should have stayed in the main part of the club. This room is way more dangerous. Now I'm alone with Leighton, and based on what is in front of me, I know what his intentions are.

I just hope Beckett and the guys are still tracking me. I'm not sure I'm in any shape to escape on my own.

8

BECKETT

My heart stopped at Caius's words, and I don't think there is any way to restart it.

Gage found out who killed Odette. He knows it's Ri. They all do, I suspect.

And Caius is about to beat my ass for hiding the truth, for Ri not already being dead.

"Who is it?" I ask, my voice cracking as I speak.

"I don't know. Gage wouldn't say. He said you deserved to know first."

I nod, but inside my nerves are shattered. I need to find Gage and put a stop to what he thinks he knows.

"I have to go ahead and help arrange for the ceremony. I'm taking Hayes with me. Lennox and Gage will go with you to the initiation ceremony," Caius says.

Lennox nods his agreement.

"Am I to expect another competition?" I ask.

Caius smirks. "No, this will be a pretty straightforward ceremony. Then once you get retribution for Odette, it will be permanent."

Permanent—as soon as I kill Ri.

Jesus, I run my hand through my hair, trying to keep the anxiety in my chest pounding through me like a herd of antelope quiet so that Caius doesn't notice my stress.

Hayes arrives, so he and Caius head out, leaving me with Lennox.

"Where's Gage?" I ask.

"In his room. He's looking over the footage he cracked one more time to be sure he knows who it is before we leave. He thought it would help you during the initiation ceremony to know who killed Odette," Lennox answers.

"Pull the car around to the front. I'll speak with Gage, and we'll be ready to go soon," I say.

Lennox nods and walks to the door to do as I asked.

I take a breath for what seems like the first time since Caius spoke as I go in search of Gage. I have no idea what I'm going to do when I find him. I just go.

Gage's room is the third door on the left. The door is open, so I don't knock. I just stand in the entryway, looking stern-faced and domineering. It doesn't matter what Gage knows. I'm the one about to be given the leadership position. I'm the one about to have all the power, not him.

I don't show my fear, my anguish, my anxiety. I don't show my turmoil at trying to figure out what to do about Ri, why I haven't already killed her. I don't show him anything but an alpha in complete control, an arrogant leader who won't bow down to anyone.

Gage is sitting on his bed with his computer in his lap.

"So you went against my orders and pulled up the video," I say, my anger flowing through my words.

"You already knew who killed Odette. You've known this whole time," Gage says, his voice flat, not giving away his emotions.

I don't answer him.

Gage closes his laptop. "I'm sorry, I was just trying to help. I didn't realize that you had already figured it out and had everything under control."

"I do have everything under control." I eye him sternly.

"Of course you do, it's just..." Gage rubs the back of his head, a bead of sweat dripping down his forehead.

"What?" I snap.

"It's Ri—that complicates things."

"And why would it complicate things?" I growl. "Ri is responsible for Odette's death. A woman I loved more than anything. I will get retribution for her death."

"What do you want me to do then?" Gage asks.

"Say nothing. Tell no one what you know."

"What about Caius and the guys? I told them I know who killed Odette."

I frown. "That was a mistake."

Gage winces at my tone.

"You will tell them that I have ordered you not to tell anyone. The information is too sensitive. If the information were to leak, it would prevent me from getting retribution. You will hide that it is Ri. Lennox, Hayes, and Caius care too much about her. If they know the truth, they might try to stop me."

"But Caius, he's my leader. I have to—"

"No. I'm your leader. I will be his leader after tonight. If you want to remain in the Retribution Kings, you will do as I say."

Gage tenses.

"Do I have your word?"

Gage pauses for a minute before finally standing. "You have my word. I won't tell anyone that it's Ri."

I don't know if I trust Gage, and I still have no idea what I'm going to do about Ri. Try to get answers. Try to understand why she did it; maybe that would help. Try to understand if she's a cold-blooded killer or if she was just doing what she was forced to do to save someone else.

Right now, though, I have to go become a leader to a group that has done nothing but betray me. For some reason I still don't understand, they want me to be their leader. No, need me. I just have to find out why. And then I'll destroy everyone who had a part in destroying my life.

———

I open the passenger door and step out of the car before Lennox even has the car stopped. I don't know what this ceremony will entail. I don't know how I will be accepted as their leader, but I want this over with. I want the power to destroy them all if I want, to decide what to do about Ri, and this is how I get it.

Lennox and Gage step out of the car, and we start walking toward the arena. It's the same arena I fought Caius in only days earlier.

And then I hear the low whistle, so quiet that it almost melds into the night air. But I know who it is and what I must do.

"You guys go ahead. I need a minute to gather my thoughts," I say.

Lennox puts his hand on my shoulder. "You're going to be great. There was a reason you were chosen. Don't doubt yourself."

Lennox walks inside. Gage only nods at me before he follows Lennox in, leaving me alone outside.

I scan the street before I take off, jogging toward the dark alleyway. I stop once the shadows hide me from the street.

"You didn't need to come, brother," I say.

"And miss my brother's initiation as leader of a different crew?" Enzo steps forward, putting his arms around me as he hugs me.

I exhale a deep breath in his embrace. For a second, all my worries disappear. It's just me and my brother.

Enzo steps back, looking at me with concern. "I've missed you. We all have."

I sigh, realizing the real reason he's come. He's here not to celebrate my triumph at becoming a leader but to try to guilt me into returning.

"I've missed everyone too. How are my nieces and nephews?"

"Everyone is well, but we're all worried about you. This made sense when you were with Odette. We even gave you time to try to get revenge for her death. But are you sure you want this?"

I frown. "Am I sure that I want to be the leader of a criminal organization that I barely understand? One that I'm sure is a rival to the one my brother controls? A job that will require tremendous responsibility and a target placed on my back for the rest of my life? Am I sure that I want this? No, I'm not sure. I didn't want any of this. That's why I chose Odette. A fresh start, a chance to live and have kids without the danger that this world puts us in."

"Then don't do this. Come back with me. Be with your family and friends. You'll find someone else to love. I know Odette was your everything, but you'll find that again."

I shake my head as my blood boils in my head.

"You know why I can't go back. I love you all too much to go back."

Enzo frowns. "You need to come back. The past is in the past. No one cares. We just want you back."

"I can't come back. I can't be forgiven for what happened."

"Not that we feel the need to forgive you, but we do forgive you for what happened."

"I don't forgive myself," I snap.

We stare back and forth at each other. Silently, letting my words set in.

"Then leave. Travel the world. Spend some time healing. Don't become the leader of a criminal organization that you will never be able to escape from."

"No amount of time will heal me. No amount of travel will make me forgive myself for what happened. The world has shown me time and time again that I don't deserve happiness. I don't get a happily ever after. I might as well do something worthy. I might as well follow through and get revenge for Odette."

Enzo sighs. "If you do this, then we are rivals. We will fight in wars against each other. We will have no choice."

"There is always a choice. As leader, I can ensure that we never go to war with each other."

Enzo's eyes grow heavy. "There's a lot you don't know about being a leader, but you'll learn."

Enzo starts to walk away. "I wish you luck, Beckett. And we will always be here for you as your family, even when the inevitable battle happens."

9

RI

I STARE at the empty room save for little more than a king-sized bed. The room is all shades of dark mahogany and even darker sheets. There is no door except for the one we just entered through. No windows, no way to escape unless I plan on fighting off his entire club. Even if I were completely healthy, it would be impossible.

I purse my lips, blowing out a slow breath. Remain calm. Showing my anger and fear will do nothing to help me escape.

"Make yourself comfortable on the bed while I make us some drinks," Leighton says.

That is the absolute last thing I want to do. "Just water for me, please."

Leighton walks over to the small bar I now notice in the corner of the room. "I insist. I thought we'd celebrate my win with a bottle of Dom Pérignon."

It's just champagne. I can handle drinking a glass without getting drunk, so I give him a sly smile of agreement. But I refuse to sit on the bed. Instead, I walk around the room, seemingly interested in the few pieces of decoration in the room. There's a dark painting on the wall of what appears to be a raven. I stare at it intently while trying to figure out my next move.

Get him drunk enough for him to pass out. That's going to be hard to do when we are only drinking champagne.

Fight him. I stare down at my arm in a sling. My odds of winning aren't great.

Fake sleep. I don't know if that would stop him.

Pop a stitch and beg him to take me back to the hospital.

None of my options are great.

My heart starts to beat louder in my chest. I put my hand over it, persuading it to settle.

I've never failed you before, heart, I won't this time either, I promise.

I feel him behind me. I want to spin and punch him in the throat. Disarm him and use his gun to shoot him, but that would draw attention. There's no telling what his men would do to me if I succeeded in killing Leighton.

He places his hand on my shoulder, and it takes everything in me not to jump out of my skin at his touch.

"Here you go," he says.

I slowly turn to see him holding out a champagne glass to me. I take the glass from him.

He grins down at me, making my insides turn. "To us. To our future. I have no doubt I'm the best man for you. I'll win the remaining games, and soon we will be husband and wife, ruling over the Corsi empire together. To us."

He raises his glass and clinks it against mine.

I stare wide-eyed at him as he drinks. His seductive eyes on mine make my skin crawl.

When he finishes his sip, he nods in my direction,

waiting for me to sip from my own glass. I force my lips around the glass and take a small sip.

Leighton's face lights up as I do as I'm told. He grabs my waist and pulls me close to him briskly. I can't do much to fight back with one arm in a sling and the other gripping my champagne glass.

But my glass is also the thing that keeps our bodies apart. He can't pull our bodies together like he wants without spilling my glass.

Still, he keeps his free hand on my waist.

"I should probably try to sleep. It's been a long day, and the doctor recommended plenty of rest for me to heal. Is there another room nearby? I'm even fine sleeping on a couch. I wouldn't want to disturb you. I'm told I'm a snorer."

He chuckles. "I doubt that very much. But even if you are, I wouldn't worry about me. I'll be sleeping next to most beautiful girl in the world. But I don't plan on sleeping."

Acid rises in my throat, and I throw the rest of my champagne back in my throat, hoping to wash my vile down. Leighton takes my glass immediately after I finish it and sets it down with his on the floor. Both of his hands find their way back to my hips as he yanks me to him.

Hip against hip, chest against chest, our breaths blaze on top of each other, but for very different reasons—his out of desire, mine out of unconfined fury.

"Leighton, please remove your hands. I'm tired. I need to sleep."

"I won you, Princess. I only get you for a week until I have to fight to win you again. I will not let a moment go to waste."

Suddenly he leans down to press his lips against mine.

I duck, kicking him in the shin as I evade the kiss. Leighton releases me, and I run to the door. Maybe if I run out of here, I'll make it out of the club before any of Leighton's men come after me.

My feet move far too slowly.

Leighton recovers quickly.

The weight of his body presses down on me from behind as he tackles me to the floor. My injured arm takes the brunt of his weight as we go down hard.

I cry out at the pain.

"I love how much of a fighter you are. I've had far too many submissive women," Leighton croons against my ear.

My arm throbs, and my lungs struggle for air as his body crushes me. But I won't give up. I'm a fighter, as he says, and I won't let him win.

My mind spins with ways to escape. My first step is getting him off of me, though.

I moan loudly, faking more pain than I'm actually in. As expected, he pushes down harder, relishing my sounds of suffering. I let my face smush into the rug, muffling my moans to keep them from him.

I can barely breathe with my face against the thick rug, but Leighton plays right into my hand. He flips me over, still pressing against me and inflicting the pain he enjoys causing.

I anticipate the move. As soon as he flips me, I slide my hand into the back of his pants and grab his gun.

I fire into his shoulder, and he falls back in a roar. I would have rather aimed for his heart or head and killed him with one bullet, but the close proximity and angles of our bodies only gave me one view.

"You bitch," he spits at me.

It's enough relief for me to make my escape.

I spring to my feet and once again run toward the door. This time I have a gun, a weapon to defend myself with. My odds of making it out of here still aren't good, but they're better now.

I underestimate Leighton, though. His ability to handle pain is greater than I realized. He's on his feet just a step behind me.

He's faster than me; I can't outrun him.

I spin, aiming my gun at him, but come face to face with the barrel of a new gun in his hand.

His grotesque smirk covers his face as blood spills from the wound in his shoulder.

"You can't shoot me. My father will kill you if you return me injured," I say with my own winning smirk.

Leighton frowns. "Maybe not until after I win you as my wife. Then, I'll make you bleed twice as much as what you've taken from me."

"Lower your gun or I'll shoot you, and this time it will be in the heart."

He raises his eyebrows at me. "I knew your father trained you. The sweet princess act was just that—an act. I knew it."

"Lower. Your. Gun."

Leighton looks me in the eyes, and what he finds must be the truth of my words. I will shoot him dead if he doesn't lower his gun. I'll probably shoot him dead either way, but I might settle just tying him up if he does as I say. He drops his gun.

"Move to the bed."

He cocks his head, not showing any sign of the pain and agony he must be in. He doesn't even grip his arm as he walks backward to the side of the bed and sits down on it.

"Tie your arm to the bed."

"Kinky," he grins. "But unfortunately for you, I don't like playing the submissive. I much prefer the dom role."

"Well, unfortunately for you, you don't have a choice." I lower the gun and aim for his crotch. "That is if you want to keep your favorite appendage."

Amusement dances in his eyes as he retrieves a rope from the top drawer of the nightstand. I knew without looking the drawer would have rope, and no doubt it was meant for me.

He begins to tie the rope around his wrist, following my orders, but the hair on my arms stands up. Something's wrong. This is too easy.

Leighton stops suddenly. "You think you've won, don't you?"

"I won't win until I'm free to marry whomever I want and choose my own future. Until then, I'll always be trapped."

He sneers, still tying the rope around his wrist, taking his time. "That will never happen. In about five minutes, you're going to be tied to this bed, and I'll be having my way with you."

"It's much more likely you'll be dead within the next five minutes. If you move at all or anyone enters this room, I'll shoot you dead."

"I won't have to move to make you do what I want." There's a sparkle in his eyes as he lays out his plan in his head.

My smile falters. "The champagne. You put something in the champagne." My head starts to spin in dread. I need to get out of here, now.

"Why would I do that when I have a much easier way of controlling you at my disposal? One that won't rob you of the lovely memories of our time together."

I freeze, thinking of all the things he could be talking about. *Who could he hurt? What could he do?*

None of my imaginations are as dreadful as what he actually does. He doesn't fight fair, and I don't even know how he does it. But one minute, I'm aiming the gun, determined to pull the trigger and blow his brain out; the next I'm lying on the bed. My arms are tied together to the headboard above. My legs are spread wide and tied to the posts on either corner with no memory of how I got here.

Leighton stares at me from the foot of the bed with a dark, unrelenting gaze.

I close my eyes, trying to block it out. I couldn't save myself. I failed. My only hope is Beckett—a man who hates playing the hero. A man I hate depending on. A man who better damn well be watching and come to my rescue. He owes me after shooting me in the arm.

Beckett will come. He owes me. *But will it be too late to save me?*

10

BECKETT

STANDING in the center of the stage with all eyes on me, I get an ominous feeling. Applause breaks out as Stan, one of the elders, speaks next to me, continuing the ceremony. Not just polite applause, but genuine, enthusiastic applause. Not days before, this crowd was cheering on Caius and booing me.

Something's not right. I just can't figure out what.

It doesn't matter. Soon I'll have the power to do what I want, to find out the exact lengths people in the Retribution Kings went to betray me and to decide what I will do to extract retribution.

The ceremony so far has been fancier than the queen of England's coronation. I wasn't expecting the elegance since there was such short notice. But there are flowers, music, and a damn crown sitting on my head like they truly believe I'm their king. It's all ridiculous if you ask me.

"And now for the vows," Stan says.

I've already said vows, *but I'm expected to say more now?* He hands me a card with the words I'm supposed to say.

The words speak of loyalty, honor, and retribution. These are the same words I've already spoken.

I speak them again, but this time when I get to the part about getting retribution for Odette, there is a time limit on it.

One month.

I have one month to get retribution to keep my power.

I finish my vows with as much conviction as I can muster.

And then Stan says, "If you break any of your vows, you will die. We will all be forced to take retribution against you." He turns to the crowd. "Do you vow to ensure Beckett Monroe upholds his vows? And if he doesn't, do you vow to seek retribution against him in the ultimate form—death?"

The crowd chants back, "We do."

Chills creep down my spine when he attaches Monroe to my name. Monroe is Odette's name, not mine. I would have gladly taken it if she were alive, but now, it feels wrong.

I don't know why I'm focusing on the new name they call me when I should be focusing on the vow just taken by this crowd. This entire room of over a hundred people will turn against me if I break my vow. A vow that ensures I kill Ri. I don't have a choice if I want to live.

Ri killed Odette, so of course, I want to kill her for what she's done.

But why don't I tell them I already know who killed her? I can do something about it right here, right now. I could extract vengeance tonight, not in a month.

I want to know why. I want to hear from Ri's lips why she took Odette from me. Then, I'll kill her without a second thought.

Yes, that's the only reason for my hesitation.

"And now for the tattoo. It is tradition for our leader to have his placed over his heart," Stan says.

Of course. A life or death vow isn't enough; I should have it marked on my skin forever.

But I'm not going to argue about a damn tattoo. I grab the back of my shirt and pull it over my head. I feel the watchful eyes of the crowd staring at my bare chest and my residual limb. They can see every scar, every broken piece of me, every demon I battle. They can see it all marked on my body.

A low female whistle cuts through the crowd.

"Someone likes what they see," Stan jokes and everyone chuckles. "I'm sure Beckett will be looking for a new wife soon enough, but let him get settled into the new role first."

New wife.

Of course, they would want me to marry again. I try to keep disgust off my face. I don't care what they want. I don't care what anyone wants. I won't be marrying ever again. I won't let myself fall in love again. I've been burned too many times.

A table is brought to the stage, and I lie down on it while a middle-aged woman pulls up a small rolling stool next to me, tattoo gun in her hand.

I don't notice a template of the tattoo. "Are you going to do this freestyle?"

She smiles at me. "I've done dozens of these tattoos. Don't worry, I won't ruin your beautiful chest. I could do this tattoo in my sleep."

I look up at the ceiling—beams and ducts and darkness so far away I can barely make them out. I focus on the nothingness as her tattoo gun marks my skin. I can barely feel the pain, even as she injects ink over my sternum and heart. I feel nothing.

I have to kill Ri or they'll kill me.

What have I gotten myself into?

Why do I hesitate at all? She should already be dead.

What am I missing?

The questions pour out of me over and over. Each piercing stab of the tattoo gun elicits more questions from me.

It's just because you've fucked her. It's not real emotion, it's just lust. *Maybe if I fuck her again, I'll get her completely out of my system?*

Or maybe she'll dig her claws deeper into my heart.

"Finished," the woman says, holding out a mirror to me.

I look down at my chest.

There's a black crown in the center of my chest, an exact replica of the ones I've seen on the rest of the guys. Somehow with the shadowing work, the crown looks scary and menacing, like it has a life of its own.

"Do you like it? Anything you want me to change?"

My entire life, but I shake my head no.

She quickly gives me a sheet of instructions about how to care for the tattoo, and then I put my shirt back on.

The crowd once again cheers as Stan concludes the ceremony. Quickly, I walk off stage.

Gage quickly finds me the second I'm off stage, walking toward me with intent.

I frown. *Is he going to disobey my orders now that I'm in charge?* It would be foolish, when I have the entire Retribution Kings at my disposal.

"This better not be about what I think it is," I growl.

"It's about Ri."

No one is close enough to hear us, although I see the rest of the guys approaching.

"Not here," I command and shoulder past him.

But he doesn't follow me. He grabs my arm, determined to tell me whatever it is that will most likely get him killed.

"She's in trouble."

11

RI

LEIGHTON'S EYES bore into me, undressing me and showing me all the horrors he plans on inflicting.

I remain perfectly still, not squirming under his gaze like I want to. I won't give him the satisfaction.

"I think you might want to get that shoulder taken care of. Wouldn't want you to bleed out and die," I say.

"So sweet, your concern for me."

I roll my eyes. I'm not the least bit concerned for him. But if he leaves to address his shoulder, it gives me time to figure out how to escape.

My hope dies when he removes his shirt, and I see a bandage already covering his wound.

How long was I out of it? Why don't I remember?

"Speechless? I expected more of a fight out of you."

I snarl. "It's hard to fight when you don't play fair. Untie me, and then we'll see who wins."

"Oh, I very much played fair. Don't be a sore loser."

"I don't think raping me is me being a sore loser."

He shrugs. "It won't feel like rape when I'm done with you. You'll be begging for more."

83

"I won't. And I promise you if you touch me, I'll kill you. It might not happen today, or tomorrow, but you'll be dead before your next birthday."

"My birthday is coming up in two weeks. You won't succeed in killing me by then." He grins.

I glare back, narrowing my eyes into dark black slits. "I will."

He prowls toward me. "I love how feisty you are. I almost want to untie you just to see you fight."

"You won't because you're a coward and you know you'd lose."

"I already won. You lost. But don't worry, the moans I plan on extracting from your pretty little mouth are going to make you think you've won."

He moves to the bedside table out of my vision, and I hear him pull something out.

My arm aches with a burning fire from being pulled up above my head. My legs are spread too wide, causing sharp pain in my hips from being overstretched. I don't know how I'm going to escape. The ropes are tied well, and it will take me a while to wiggle out of them. But if I so much as try, Leighton will tie them tighter or add additional ropes.

It's hopeless.

And then I feel the cool graze of metal against my stomach, and I see what Leighton pulled from the drawer —a knife. He runs the blade through my shirt, ripping it in half as he makes his way all the way up. The edge of the blade scratches my skin, leaving a shallow trail of blood from my stomach to between my breasts.

"Oops," Leighton grins. "You're so beautiful when you bleed, though."

I don't react. I don't give him the satisfaction. I just

remember every little thing he does. Every drop of blood he spills. Every crude joke. Every sly grin. I'll remember every violation and use it all against him. I'll make sure he pays for every ounce of pain he causes me.

But I won't let it destroy me. I'm too strong for that.

When he's finished ripping my shirt and bra in half, he moves down to my pants.

I close my eyes as I feel the blade against my lower stomach. I'm not sure I can handle him ripping my pants off.

If I can't bear that, how am I going to endure the rest?

He suddenly stops after barely making a cut more than an inch at the top.

I open one cautious eye and see that he's digging in his own pocket for his phone.

"This better be important," Leighton snaps into the phone.

He listens carefully; his face turning darker by the minute.

"This is unacceptable." He pauses. "Of course, I'll be there. And everyone who had any part in this will pay."

He practically throws his phone back into his pocket and snatches his shirt up off the bed. He almost walks out the door without even talking to me, when he stops and turns suddenly.

"I'll be back soon, to continue this later. I'd love to see you try to escape, but I don't expect you'll get very far." He runs his hand through his hair. His hungry gaze eats every inch of my bare skin.

I want to curl and hide from his stare, but I just remember. I remember every foul look.

He'll pay.

"I'll be quite angry when I get back and will need to let

off some steam. It will make our time together much more enjoyable."

And then he walks out the door.

I can't believe my good luck. I don't know how long he'll be gone, though, and I have to get out of these ropes as fast as possible. I'm sure he has guards posted outside the door, but that will be my second problem. First, I need to get these damn ropes off.

I squirm, working the rope that cuts into my wrists and trying to loosen them.

Five minutes pass, and I haven't made much progress. All I've accomplished is giving myself a bad rope burn and rubbed my skin raw until it's bleeding. I don't know how Leighton tied these, but it's tighter than I realized. It's going to take me a while to get out of these—too long.

The lights flicker and then turn off.

I instinctively let out a screech before snapping my mouth closed. I don't need to draw attention to myself if it's just a quick power outage. If anything, this could provide me a distraction to sneak away in the night.

Something moves in the shadows, and I freeze. My breath catches in my throat. My eyes can barely make out the movement in the dark.

Who's there?

Leighton?

One of his men?

But then I see him—a man who has haunted my dreams with his dark grey eyes and crooked grin. A man worse than Leighton is standing at the foot of my bed.

What is he doing here? What does he want?

He's the only man I truly fear—the only man who can truly beat me.

I shiver, I can't help it.

Suddenly, the lights snap on. I stare at the foot of the bed, but there is no man there. He's gone.

My head falls back, and I exhale a deep breath. I can't hesitate for long. I need to figure out how to escape. But first, I need to settle my speeding heart so I can focus.

It was just a dream. I just imagined it. He wasn't real.

"You really have a way of getting trapped in the worst predicaments, don't you?" The voice snaps me out of myself, and I look around the room, until I find Beckett leaning against the wall near the bed.

Just like Leighton, he towers over me and stares down at my body with a heady gaze. But unlike when Leighton looks at me, I crave more. I want that greedy stare. I want him admiring my body. I want him wanting me.

But that's not what he's doing with his stare. He's trying to figure out how damaged I am. How injured. How broken.

I hate it.

I don't want him or anyone to ever see me as broken. I'm strong. I'm a fighter. I'm not weak.

"Stop looking at me like that. Either help untie me or leave me alone."

He doesn't move. Not to help. Not to leave.

I go back to trying to get the rope undone at my wrists, but it hurts so fucking much. My bicep is killing me, and I quickly give up.

"Really? You're not going to help me."

He raises an eyebrow. "I already helped you."

I frown. "I'm still tied to this bed. I don't see how you've helped me so far."

"I had the guys cause a distraction. They set their building that holds their weapons and drugs on fire. Leighton had to go deal with it. You're welcome."

I roll my eyes. "I'll thank you when you untie me."

He tilts his head, still studying me like he expects me to burst into tears at any moment.

I don't. I won't.

"Did he..." Beckett asks, his voice breaking.

I know what he's asking. *Did Leighton touch me? Did he rape me? Was Beckett too late?*

"Like you care."

The softness in his gaze, the torment in his eyes, the twinge at the corner of his lips say he does care. He's here. He saved me when I had no one else.

His eyes scan my body more thoroughly, looking for a sign since I won't tell him what happened. His gaze is a gentle caress as he examines my bare breasts, the rip in my shirt, and the one at the top of my pants.

"I'm fine. Leighton barely touched me before you sent the distraction."

Beckett nods solemnly.

"Are you going to untie me now?"

Beckett doesn't answer me. "What is this note?"

I stare at the piece of paper in his hand with a frown. "I have no idea what it is."

"It was lying at the foot of the bed when I arrived."

The shadows, the ghost, the man—he was real.

I shiver as Beckett unfolds the note and begins to read.

"'You failed. Too many know the truth.'" Beckett stops and looks at me. "What does this mean?"

I shrug. "I have no idea."

He holds my gaze, looking firmly in my eyes like he can read my thoughts, down to my very soul. With an intense heat in his eyes, he says, "I think you do."

12

BECKETT

I DON'T KNOW who left this note, but someone else is on to her. Someone else knows she's lying and has been hiding who she truly is. She's not a trapped princess being held in a tower until her father marries her off. She's an accomplished mastermind, playing equally by her father's side.

I'm tired of waiting for answers. We have plenty of time before Leighton returns, and the guys will let me know as soon as he leaves.

I need answers.

I walk closer to the bed Ri's tied to. I want to do nothing more than climb on top of her and fuck her until all the memories of Leighton flee her head, and all she can think about is me. My kisses and licks against her hot flesh, my cock sliding between her slick folds.

That's what I want. It's what she wants.

But neither of us will get that ever again.

No, I need answers. I need to understand. And then I need to end her life for what she did to Odette.

There is no reason to wait any longer. I need to do it, and then I can be free. I will have the power of an empire behind me. I'll live the rest of my life as a bachelor. I've yet to decide if I will destroy the Retribution Kings from within or let them thrive under my control, but that's for another day. Today is about getting revenge for Odette.

"Tell me about the day we met. Why did you run through my wedding?"

"Why do you care? Why now?"

"Just answer the question."

"I was running from the same man who left that note."

"Or were you working with him?"

Her eyebrows raise, and her body arches on the bed as she tugs on the rope tying her up. So beautiful and strong and feisty. But not mine, never mine.

"No, I wasn't working with him. I was running from him. But that's not going to stop you from accusing me. From the first time we met, you've seen me as your enemy. You've blamed me for ruining your wedding, for taking you away from your wife, so you weren't there to protect her when she was taken and killed. But I'm not your enemy, Hero."

"Then what are you?" My voice comes out as almost a whisper, as if I don't want to know the truth.

"I'm the woman who saves you when no one else will." She pauses. "And you're the man who saves me. You can pretend we need bargains and bets and reasons to save each other, but we both know we'd do it for free."

She's right. I hate seeing her hurt. It's killing me to leave her tied up. I thought it would help me get answers from her, but all it does is stir the alpha male inside me who wants to protect her. Who wants to make her mine. Who wants to devour every inch of her and take away every drop of pain.

She killed Odette.

Killed my wife.

The love of my life.

She did it.

I watched it with my own eyes.

But watching Ri tied to another man's bed, the sincerity in her eyes, the flush of her skin makes me forget my rage at her. It's all turned on Leighton.

Ri may deserve to die for what she did to Odette, but she doesn't deserve this. No one does.

I rush to the top of the bed to untie her arms as quickly as possible. It was wrong of me to keep her tied in fear when I could do something about it, even to get answers.

I reach up with my knife, intending to slice through the ropes.

"Wait," Ri says.

I stop, looking down at her and listening carefully at the door, assuming she heard someone coming. But I don't hear anything. Not a sound except for her heavy breath against my neck.

"What is it?"

She leans up, her body arching fully off the bed until her lips brush over mine. It's a light and tender kiss. A kiss to wash away any demons she's dealing with.

I try to leave it at that—a soft, gentle kiss. But the second her lips brush against mine, everything changes. My body hardens, my anger dissipates, and my lust takes over all of my thoughts. I become an animal set on devouring her.

She moans in response against my lips, recognizing the difference in me.

"Tell me to stop, to cut the ropes and leave," I pant over her lips.

"I can't because it's not what I want. I want to give a big fuck you to Leighton by fucking another man in this bed. I want to erase each of his touches, his threats. I want you to push out all the demons he shoved inside me." She pauses. "But most of all, I want you."

She wants me.

I can see the desire and hunger in her eyes. Sure, she wants to stick it to Leighton. For the room to smell like sex, the sheets to be messy and covered in the results of our love-making. But the reason above all others is that she wants me.

A shit-eating grin forms on my face, while my insides are screaming warnings at me. Ri wants me. *What if she killed Odette because she saw me and decided she wanted me? And that the easiest way to get me single was to kill my wife?*

But she bites her lower lip, and my eyes drift down her heated body from her face to her exposed breasts and bare stomach. All those thoughts vanish from my head in an instant.

She wants me.

I want her.

We shouldn't do this here. Leighton's men are just outside. Leighton himself could return at any moment. But when my eyes meet hers again, I know there is no stopping us. The danger just heightens every feeling. It won't stop us.

I look up at her arms tied above her head. Her injured arm must be throbbing with pain. I'm surprised she's not near delirious with agony from it.

I drop my knife and run my index finger slides down her arms from her wrists to her bicep. My nail sends delicious shivers through her body and extracts a soft moan from her.

"I should untie these," I say, looking at the ropes.

"No," she begs.

I kiss her, unable to resist her pink lips. Our tongues tangle together, and I climb on top of her, my legs on either side of her hips as I deepen the kiss. I only pull away when her moans grow so loud that I'm afraid someone will hear outside.

"You sure, Fighter? Because I don't plan on being gentle."

Her eyes twinkle. "I don't either."

I growl in response.

What is this woman doing to me? Why do I want her so desperately?

I can barely think, barely breathe when I'm around her. I try to think about how it was with Odette. *Was it like this? Did I need to be inside her more than I needed my heart to beat? More than I needed oxygen in my lungs? More than I needed to live?*

No, it wasn't like this.

But this isn't love. It's just lust. I still hate her. I just need to get her out of my system one last time. And when I get my retribution, I need to know that she's whole and not thinking about what Leighton did to her.

My lips smash against hers, making it near impossible for either of us to breathe. Neither of us care, though. The desire pulsing through us is too overwhelming, too much for either of us to handle or think clearly.

"I love seeing you tied up and completely at my mercy," I say, kissing down her neck.

"You think because I'm tied up that I'm at your mercy?"

I suck her earlobe, and she trembles. "I know it."

And then I prove my point by kissing and licking my way down her neck. I continue lower and kiss the top curve of her breast, watching as her body writhes beneath me, begging me to lick and suck her sensitive nipple. But I'm not ready yet. I want to take my time with her. This will, after all, be the last time.

I kiss the swell of her other breast, and she wiggles against the ropes holding her wrists above her head.

"You're driving me crazy," Ri says.

I smile as I kiss down the center of her belly, avoiding the most sensitive parts of her. I want her begging and soaked and screaming my name before I even enter her.

"I know. And you're about to lose your mind." I dip my hand to the fastener of her pants, but I quickly realize with her legs tied apart, I'm not going to be able to remove them intact.

Her heavy gaze reads my thoughts.

"Do it," she says.

I pull out a knife from my back pocket. I kiss her lower stomach one more time before running the blade through her pants.

There's a tinge of fear in her eyes as her thoughts drift back to what Leighton did to her.

I won't allow that pain in any further. The second her pants are down to her mid-thighs, my head dips between her thighs, finding the most sensitive spot on her body and pulling the bud between my lips, sucking hard.

She cries out—far too loudly.

I quickly finish cutting her pants off as I suck, keeping one eye on the door behind us, prepared for Leighton's men to come in and check on her.

The door never opens, but we can't keep pushing our luck.

I stop sucking as soon as I get her pants off.

"Don't stop," she pants.

I sit up, straddling her body again as I cock my head to one side with a wicked grin. "I can't if you keep screaming like that."

"I can't be quiet, not with you."

"Then you don't get to have me," I say.

She narrows her eyes into a look of determination and teasing punishment, as if to threaten withholding herself from me in retaliation.

My cock stiffening in my pants reminds me that that's not an option. I need her even if we don't make it out of here alive.

I hover over her breast. "If you make a sound, I'll stop."

I let my tongue flick over her nipple.

She cries out, arching her back and pressing her breast further into my mouth.

I frown as I stop. This isn't going to work.

"Do you trust me?" I ask, my hand lightly massaging her other full breast in my hand. I'm unable to stop even as more soft whimpers rumble through her throat.

She nods.

Stupid girl. She shouldn't trust me. I don't even trust myself to know what's right. Our unending lust for each other is going to be the death of us.

I lean over her to the drawer in the nightstand next to the bed and cringe at what I find—all sorts of instruments that could have been used to inflict pain on her. Whips, knives, matches, butt plugs, handcuffs, and some I can't even identify, but I find what I'm looking for.

I pull out the duct tape and hold it up to her.

Her eyes widen, but then she licks her lips. "I'll do anything if it means I get to feel you inside me as we both come."

"We need a safe gesture, something that I know means stop if I go too far."

"No, I trust you. You'll recognize it if you go too far."

I nod because I will. I know her too well not to notice the signs. Whether I'm actually strong enough to stop is the real question.

I lower my lips to hers, kissing her one last time before putting the piece of tape over her mouth. The kiss isn't enough. It sparks something dark and devious inside me. Something primal and all alpha male like—*she's mine.*

Mine.

Mine.

Mine.

And I'm going to fuck her here in another man's bed to prove to him and everyone else that she's mine. It doesn't matter what they do, she belongs to me. She's mine to fuck. Mine to save. Mine to care for. Mine to kill.

All mine.

I stand off the bed, looking at her completely naked body spread for me. She squirms under my gaze, her eyes begging me to fuck her—now.

I chuckle at how bossy she is even tied up. She demands control.

But I need a moment to drink her in, to regain some of my own control. How foolish of me, though. I can't control myself, not with her.

I remove my shirt, then pants and boxers. She's naked, and I want to feel every inch of her skin against mine.

I walk back to the bed, my hand trailing down her body to between her legs.

"You're soaked. So ready for me."

She nods, squeezing her eyes shut like she's going to combust if I don't fuck her already.

"So strong." I climb up on the bed, settling between her spread legs and enjoying the perfect view of her glorious pussy.

I kiss her cheek, then her neck. "So beautiful."

I take her nipple in, then the other. "So determined."

And then I kiss between her legs, easily finding her clit and sucking it roughly into my mouth.

She moans and writhes, but the moan is muted compared to what it was before. It's soft enough that I'm not worried about others hearing us.

I could spend all day devouring her, tasting her sweet juices, licking over her clit until she's vibrating with ecstasy. But we don't have the time, so I'll have to settle for just making her come, then sliding inside her and pulling another orgasm from her.

Her first orgasm comes far too quickly. I slide my fingers inside of her soaked pussy as I suck on her swollen clit. She moans, but it's the way she clamps down hard on my fingers that lets me know she's coming apart.

When my eyes peek up at her, I see her eyes rolled back in her head as her entire body seems to convulse with the orgasm.

I smirk as I settle between her legs, my cock impatient as I spend another second just watching her. But the look she flashes me is one that says if I don't sink inside her right now, she'll find a way to get these ropes off and tie me up so she can have her way with me.

I grab her hips and let myself sink into her like we both want.

I groan before remembering that I have to be quiet.

"I should have duct-taped my mouth shut too," I say, barely moving so I don't explode inside of her before I even start.

She smiles beneath the tape, her eyes glowing.

I gently rock, panting as I do.

Her eyes don't leave mine as I begin to fuck her, thrusting deeper and deeper inside her, filling her so completely. I don't know why this feels so good, but it does —so fucking good.

And then I speak to her before I lose all my thoughts. "Leighton won't have succeeded. You wouldn't have let him. You're stronger than him. Smarter. You would have found a way to make him stop. But if, for some reason, he did succeed, you're strong enough to deal with anything. And I would be there right by your side ensuring that you got retribution."

A tear dribbles out of the corner of her eye.

I reach up with my lips and kiss it away.

For just a moment, we share a soul. Something strange happens, and I don't hate her. For only a second, I let my irrational mind take over. It tells me she didn't kill Odette, even though I saw it with my own eyes.

I thrust again, and all thoughts are gone, from both of us. The entire bed rattles as I thrust and thrust, biting my bottom lip to keep from screaming.

My thumb finds her clit, and then I'm starting to come undone. I'm not going to be able to hold it in. My climax is building to uncontrollable levels. I muted her moans, but I should have done the same to myself.

I'm one millisecond away from screaming at the top of my lungs and not caring who hears me, when Ri suddenly gets one of her arms free. I don't know how she does it, but she's fucking incredible.

I can barely process her movements they are so fast, and my brain is barely functioning.

The tape is gone from her mouth, and her hand wraps

around the base of my neck, jerking me to her, just as I explode inside her.

Our muffled screams catch in each other's mouths, rattle around in each other's throats. There is no doubt we are screaming each other's names. This intense reaction only happens with each other.

I don't remember feeling this way before, not with Odette, not ever.

The emotions that flood through me are beyond intense. They are overwhelming, and I have no idea what to do with them.

As I pull away, I have a huge grin on my face. That is until I hear the door open. Apparently, we weren't quite enough.

13

———

RI

It—it was...

Beckett was...

Jesus, I'm speechless. I have no words to convey how being with Beckett felt.

None.

And I don't have time to process what just happened. Two of Leighton's men have burst through the door, and I doubt it will take long for more to come pouring in.

I'm completely naked. My legs are still tied to the bed, as is my injured arm. Beckett is on top of me, naked as well. We have no weapons within our reach. We're fucked.

Beckett's face turns dark immediately, but he glances back to me, and I can see the conflict in his eyes. He doesn't want to leave me naked and still tied to the bed, but he doesn't have a choice.

I give him a quick nod to go.

His frown deepens, his brows pinching together, and he turns and jumps off the bed just as the two men approach.

He throws a punch, hitting the first man hard. The muscles in his back contract and ripple as he moves. I get lost in them, just staring at his rippled back. I'm bitting my bottom lip and practically drooling as I watch my naked man fight the two men.

"You going to help, Fighter? Or should I go back to calling you Princess?" Beckett says as he knocks one of the men to the floor.

A blush takes over my body, but I quickly go to work untying my other arm and legs. I've undone my arm and one leg, when I feel a shirt hit me. It's Beckett's shirt, I realize, as the scent hits me.

"No one else gets to see what's mine," Beckett says as he winks at me and takes a blow to the stomach.

Then I notice he threw me more than just his shirt. There's a knife between the thin fabric.

I quickly put the shirt on and grab the knife casually at my side as one of the men approaches me. I don't hesitate, jabbing the knife into his chest, and blood spurts all over my hands. I quickly withdraw the knife as his body grows heavy against the knife, and he drops to the floor.

My heart flutters as Beckett's words sink in—*mine*. I wish it were true, but I don't believe him, not yet.

More men start rushing into the room with guns drawn. We are vastly outnumbered, especially with only one knife between the two of us. My arm is still injured. Beckett is still naked. The odds aren't in our favor.

I glance at Beckett out of the corner of my eye, and he winks at me. We're in this together. We can do this. We are stronger together than a dozen men.

I jump off the bed with my knife in my hand. I don't care that the first man I approach has a gun. He aims it for me with a shaky hand, but I know he has orders not to shoot me or I'd already be shot. The gun is useless against me.

I don't bother knocking the gun out of his hand; I simply duck beneath his hands as I jab the knife up into his stomach. The groan he makes is low but loud. I've been taught self-defense my whole life. I've killed men, but every time I do, the sounds are what stay with me. The guttural noises haunt me later.

I pull the knife out before stabbing him again in the chest, assuring him a swift death. He moans one last time before falling to the floor with a thud. I turn to watch Beckett turn a gun on the man he's fighting, shooting him in the gut.

Beckett takes the gun and shoots two more men closest to him, each shot straight in the head between the eyes with perfect aim.

"Want the gun?" Beckett asks me as I approach him.

"Nah, you're a better shot, and I prefer the knife."

He smirks down at me. "Was that a compliment?"

"Don't let it go to your head." I take a step in front of Beckett as a man aims his gun as us, but Beckett's quicker.

"What are you doing? Get behind me," he commands.

"No, they won't shoot me. If they did, Leighton or my father would kill them. But they won't have any problem shooting you."

"And they won't have any problem trying to aim for me and accidentally shooting you in the process," Beckett growls.

"Are you concerned about my well-being? I thought you didn't care about me?" I tease.

He narrows his eyes on me. "So stubborn, Princess."

I frown, annoyed that he called me Princess, and he knows it.

But we don't have time to be pissed at each other. I throw my knife, hitting a man in the center of his chest, then grab Beckett's gun from him as he's still trying to get me to move behind him. I shoot at another man, hitting his head. The impact isn't perfectly between the eyes like Beckett's, but it does the job.

"Not bad, but you can do better," Beckett teases.

I grin, and we both run forward, attacking at full speed. Beckett doesn't ask me to hide behind him anymore. I love that he cares, but I also love that he believes in my abilities. I love—*shit, I shouldn't be thinking about love.*

Love is the last thing that should be on my mind. Survival is all I can think about. Figuring a way out of the game my father started. Maybe then I can think about love. But not now.

I shoot two more men as Beckett tackles a man to the ground and wrestles for the man's gun, but he isn't able to get the gun completely free. The man turns the gun toward Beckett's body. All he has to do is pull the trigger, and Beckett would be hit hard in the chest—seriously injured, if not dead.

My gun has one bullet left in it, and there are three men approaching me. It doesn't matter; I know what I have to do. What I want to do.

I fire the bullet straight into Beckett's attacker's forehead with perfect aim. The man falls back, releasing Beckett immediately.

I exhale, my entire body relaxing as I see Beckett unharmed. I'm so consumed with Beckett that I forget about the men still approaching me, the danger I haven't yet disarmed.

"Ri!" Beckett yells, trying to knock me out of the spell

I'm under.

It's too late. I feel a man's hand around my neck. Another hand goes around my wrist, yanking it back. I drop the useless gun and try to swing my remaining free hand around to attack the man holding me when I hear a gun fire.

The man's grip on me loosens as I realize Beckett shot him. Another shot is fired, and a second man goes down. But the third is mine.

His eyes are dark and determined. He doesn't move, simply aiming his gun at me.

Beckett and I may have been the underdogs when we started, but now, he's the one who is outnumbered. And he will lose.

I expect Beckett to shoot him dead before I get close to the man, but he doesn't. He must realize the change in my body. I want to be the one to end this. I need to end this. I need to know I'm strong enough to fight and win on my own. Beckett won't always be here to save me.

"On your knees, Princess," the man says, aiming the gun at my heart.

"Or you'll shoot me? You won't. Leighton would kill you if you did."

He shakes his head. "I don't plan on killing you, just injuring you. I'll kill your friend, though."

I scoff, looking at his gun, at the way he's holding it, his stance, even the way his eyes dilate. He's young and inexperienced. He's pretending like he knows exactly what he's doing, but I'd guess he's a poor shot, mediocre at best.

"If that were the case, he'd already be dead, and I'd be retied to that bed," I say and make my move. I dive toward him, keeping a close eye on his gun. There's no telling what the idiot is going to do.

He fires just as I tackle him to the ground. It seemed wide, but I can't be sure that he didn't hit Beckett until I turn around. And I can't do that until I kill this man—a man who works for the devil. A monster who tied me up and planned on raping me. This man may not have participated, but he's who I'm taking my wrath out on until I can kill the devil himself.

The truth is I have too many devils in my life, too many I have to kill to be truly free. And as much as I want to do it all myself, I'll need Beckett's help.

But that can wait.

I knock the gun from his hand easily. This one isn't going to have a quick death. I'm too angry. Too pissed off. Too—I can't admit what I really am. There's a new fear that Leighton sparked inside me. I've always been able to take care of myself, protect myself, keep myself safe.

But this time—no matter what Beckett says, this time I wouldn't have been able to save myself. I wouldn't have been able to get free. That is what scares me. I'm not invincible. Despite all my training, there will come a time when it isn't enough.

I punch the final man in the face, watching blood splatter from the corner of his lip. That little bit of blood gives me an endless bloodthirst. I want to spill every drop of blood from his body before I kill him.

I hit him again. He tries to punch me in the face. I duck easily and hit him harder. He doesn't get to fight. He doesn't get to win. He just gets to take all the pain boiling in me.

I throw a punch in his gut and listen to the glorious sound of his groan as pain wrenches through his body. I do it again, and again, and again—harder and harder until he can't catch his breath.

And then I go back to his face. I hit him over and over. His bones crunch under the force of my punches.

I close my eyes as I keep punching. My breathing is erratic. I'm erratic. I can't control my movements. I just hit and hit and hit. My heart rate races. My panting quickens. And then I feel the wet sting of tears on my cheeks.

I don't remember where I am or what I'm doing. I just know that the hitting feels good, that I need this. I keep punching until I'm sobbing uncontrollably, until I'm at my breaking point, about to fall over a cliff.

That's when I feel an arm wrapping around me from behind. I don't stop trying to throw punches, though. I've been hitting for so long that my body can't stop. I'm a freight train speeding full force ahead, unable to stop at a moment's notice. But my arms start flailing around instead of contacting bloody skin. Finally, my arms slow to barely a twitch and then eventually completely collapse at my sides.

But the tears don't stop. They fall and fall and fall. Every emotion explodes out with them, until I'm trembling from the adrenaline and rage.

The arm around me tightens until my head falls back against a bare chest. As my head rests against his beating heart, everything slows. His breathing and beat of his heart are so relaxed, so calm. It's impossible for my own not to match his.

He doesn't speak. He doesn't move beyond just holding me.

It's exactly what I need—a quiet space to just exist, to let all the emotions fall away.

No words.

No questions.

Just slow, steady breathing.

He won't speak first. He'll wait here forever with me until I say something. Words are hard, though. I don't know what I should say.

I glance back at him from the corner of my eyes. His strong, muscled legs are on either side of me. As my gaze travels up his thigh and I don't find any clothes, I remember that he's naked.

"You should probably put some clothes on before we leave, or we're not going to have to just worry about Leighton but every hot-blooded woman on the street chasing after us."

His laugh is delayed but full-bodied. I can feel it rattling through his chest and into my back. It makes me grin widely until I'm laughing too. It's a different kind of release, but exactly what we both need.

I look back at Beckett, and there's this intense connection, a shared experience. And dare I say it—a loving look meets mine.

But then he's clearing his throat. "We should get going. We don't know if any of the men contacted Leighton before we killed them. He could be on his way here right now."

I nod, knowing he's right. But I'm also afraid that as soon as we get up, reality is going to sink in. He's going to go back to acting like he can't stand me, and I'm going to go back to being entirely on my own.

I force myself to stand and extend my hand to him. He takes it, and I help him up. There is a deep scowl on his face as he stares at our joined hands.

"Is holding my hand that unbearable to you?" I ask, not hiding the disdain in my voice as I try to pull my hand from his grasp.

He grips my hand harder. "I'm just mad at myself for not having the tools to address your split open knuckles."

I stare down at our joined hands. My knuckles are indeed bloodied, the skin split open in gaping wounds. "It doesn't hurt."

He frowns before he leans down and brushes the softest of kisses against them.

I suck in a gasp at the featherlight touch tingling through my body.

How can he be so caring one moment and so heartless the next?

I rake my eyes down his body, partly to ensure he isn't injured and partly because I can't pass up a chance to take in every inch of his beautiful body. His muscles tighten and expand with every breath. I skim down further, enjoying the growth of his cock between his legs. Even with everything that just happened, he's straining for me, wanting me. I don't see any wounds, but my gaze goes back to the center of his chest, where a bandage is taped over the center of his chest.

"What's this?" I ask, my hand grasping at the edges.

He doesn't speak but just nods as I begin to pull at the corner. He doesn't react as I slowly peel back the bandage.

I gasp when I see it.

A large tattooed crown sits on the center of his chest. I know what that means.

"You're initiated? You're the leader? The boss?"

Beckett nods.

"Did you get retribution for Odette?"

The silence stretches until I'm not sure he's going to answer me.

Finally, he says, "I'm very close."

BECKETT

I'M NOT close to getting retribution for Odette, not close at all. I'm more confused than ever. I can't understand how Ri would have taken part in Odette's death, even to save herself. It's not something Ri would do.

If I'm going to kill Ri for what she did, I need to get to the truth. Maybe the man who left her this note has the answer. I just need to find him; Gage can help me.

Ri tosses me my pants, breaking me from my thoughts.

I put them on as she puts on her own pants. Her cheeks blush as I catch her staring at me. It strokes my ego to see how she looks at my body when very few can get past my disfiguration. But I can't let my emotions overwhelm me, or I'll have her back in that bed, fucking her until Leighton comes home.

Ri starts to remove her shirt.

"No, keep it. It looks good on you," I say.

She tucks her hair behind her ear. It's a wild mess, but it suits her—wild, and strong, and free.

"What will you wear?"

"Pants will be enough to fend off the flirtatious women until I get home," I wink at her.

She chuckles. "I'll try not to get jealous of anyone who pines after you."

Her unspoken motivation hangs in the air. She thinks of me as hers.

Just like I think of her as mine.

Ri is mine. I just have to decide what to do with her—keep her or kill her.

Tonight made everything so much more complicated. Seeing her tied up enraged me. Fucking her melted me. And watching her fight—god, that destroyed me.

Watching her fight turned on every alpha male instinct in me. I wanted to protect her with a fierceness I've never felt before. I wanted to fight every man coming our way while she ran away to safety. And yet, watching her fight and seeing the strength and skill she wields, made my cock harder than it's ever been in my life.

I thought the best way to start a family was by finding a woman not in this dangerous world, but every time I try I fail. *Maybe I should have been looking for the strongest woman in this criminal life?* That's what my brother and friends did.

I stare at Ri, a woman I could have loved. *But by goading her father to have these games, did I ruin everything? Or did she already ruin what could have been by killing Odette?*

"Ready?" she asks.

I nod.

We each pick up a gun from the corpses on the ground and then walk out of the bedroom and through the now empty club. We are just about to the front door when Ri stops.

"What about the security cameras? We need Leighton and Vincent to think I broke free on my own. I don't want you getting in trouble for this."

I put my gun in my waistband and take my phone out of my pocket. I send a quick text to Gage, and two seconds later, he texts back that he's on it.

"Gage will take care of it," I reassure her.

She nods. "Let's get out of here, then."

We disappear into the darkness, but it won't be dark for much longer. Soon the sun will be rising, and the blood on our bodies won't be easily hidden in the shadows. We'll be long gone before then, though.

"This way. I parked the car a couple of blocks from here."

She puts her gun in her waistband, and I take her hand in mine. A warm feeling rushes through my body at her single touch. It feels right to be holding her hand, like we are partners, even though we are far from on the same side. We just use each other. And soon, one of us will kill the other. It's inevitable.

But for the moment, I just enjoy her touch as I lead her to the car. Both of us are on high alert for Leighton, his men, or worse—Corsi's men catching us breaking the rules of the game.

We make it to the car in five minutes, and then I'm driving toward Caius's apartment. We'll have to sneak in so as not to be seen on any cameras that Corsi or Leighton could hack, but we're safe.

Our shoulders slump, and soft smiles stretch over our lips as we drive wordlessly. As I pull into Caius's parking garage, Gage texts me.

I glance at it.

"Gage took care of the footage at Leighton's place. He

wants us to the stairs instead of the elevator here, since there aren't any cameras. He'll take care of the footage in the hallway as we approach Caius's door."

Ri nods.

We are both exhausted. The last thing we want to do is climb a dozen staircases up, but that is exactly what we will do.

When we reach the base of the stairs, I say, "Want a piggyback ride?"

She scoffs. "Race me? Last one up owes the other one *anything*."

The inflection on 'anything' is the same we've used for every other one of our little games. Each competition brings me joy, and I'll never pass up an opportunity to have her owe me.

She's already taken off and is started up the stairs by the time I realize what she's said. She already has almost an entire flight of stairs ahead of me.

I take off running after her. I catch up to her at the second flight. I can hear her light giggles under her breath as she feels me catching up to her.

"You better run faster, or you're not going to have a shot at winning," I say.

She picks up speed, more determined than ever to beat me.

I'm hot on her heels, though. I could easily pass her, but I'm too afraid she'll pass out from blood loss or exhaustion after everything she's been through in the last twenty-four hours. She'll do anything to win.

"When I win, I'm going to make you do filthy, dirty things. Things you are going to crave from then on out," I tease.

She gulps, almost stumbling on a step before she runs

again. "As much as I'd enjoy that, I'm going to win so I can make you admit a secret to me."

I frown. That's how I should use my debt if I win, but watching her ass sway as she runs up the stairs has my brain on far dirtier things. If it wouldn't put our lives at risk to fuck in the stairwell, I'd have her again right here.

"Run faster," I growl.

She turns her head, confused at me.

I pinch her ass to get her moving and because I can't resist touching her.

She squeals. "You bastard."

But it gets the job done, and she picks up the pace.

Climbing the stairs is exhausting, and I can feel Ri losing speed. She's going to be dead by the time she reaches the top. Her breathing is ragged, sweat is running down the back of her neck, and I'm sure her heart rate and blood pressure are through the roof.

I can't stand it any longer.

I speed up to her and scoop her up before she can protest.

I wait for the wailing, the beating of her hand against my chest, or the demands to put her down. They don't come.

I keep jogging up the stairs with her cradled against me.

"Thank you," she mumbles between heavy breaths.

I hold her closer.

"Don't thank me. I'm considering this a win for me. I'm not letting you out of the bet."

She smiles up at me. "Good."

My cock hardens, and a knowing smirk dances on her lips.

I carry her the rest of the way up while Ri stares at the muscles on my chest and arm.

"You were holding back, weren't you?" she asks.

"I couldn't pass up an opportunity to stare at your ass." I wink at her, and she groans, making it even harder for me to not stop right here and fuck her against the wall, the railing, the stairs—anywhere I can have her.

I resist every urge in my body and carry her into Caius's apartment after we exit the stairs.

"Where is everyone?" she asks.

"Trying to keep Leighton and his men occupied. They'll be back soon."

I carry her into the hallway bathroom and set her down on the counter. She's still staring at my chest like she wants to devour me.

"Stop looking at me like that," I say.

"Why?"

I look down at her hands. "Because I need to play doctor for a minute, and I can't concentrate if you keep looking at me like I'm your favorite dessert."

"But you are my favorite dessert." She licks her lips.

God, help me.

I find a first aid kit in the cabinet over the toilet and open it on the counter next to where she's sitting. I pull out some antiseptic and gauze and begin cleaning her knuckles.

We don't talk as I work. She just watches intently as I clean her knuckles and wrap them in a bandage.

She moves her arm, and that's when I see the bandage on her bicep covering the bullet wound that I caused. I can't stop staring at it, torturing myself over it.

"I forgive you," she says suddenly.

I look up at her in surprise as I stand between her spread legs.

"I forgive you. I don't care why you did it. You'll probably never tell me the truth, but it doesn't matter. I forgive you."

I squeeze my eyes shut. "You shouldn't forgive me."

"It's not up to you."

I take a deep breath, my eyes still closed, unsure of what to do next. *Should I tell her? Should I show her the video of her killing Odette and ask her to explain herself?*

Before I can decide what to do, she decides her next move. Her lips brush onto mine, her tongue sweeps into my mouth, and I'm lost to her kiss. Her kiss pleads me to stay in the present, to not go back to our contentious dynamic. Her kiss begs me to be on her side, to choose her, to love her.

Love her—that's what she wants. *But how could I love her when she killed the love of my life?*

I step back, breaking the kiss, forcing us to face reality. I know what I have to do.

"I'm giving you one chance, just one." I look into her dark brown eyes beneath the thick eyelashes she's batting at me in confusion. I grip her waist as I step closer.

"I'm giving you one chance to tell me anything. Any mistake you made. Anything you've done wrong. Any harm you've caused me, my friends, my family. You can tell me anything you did, no matter the reason. Come clean, and I won't hold it against you. I won't punish you."

She cocks her head in more confusion. "I don't understand what you're talking about. What do you think I did?"

I shake my head, not wanting her to know what I know. She could run, flee, or tell her father to eliminate me because I know the truth. No, I have to keep the information to myself until I decide to kill her for her sins.

"This is your one get out of jail free card. Tell me the truth and I won't harm you. I'll help you."

She shakes her head slowly. Her hands are resting on my shoulders. "I would never hurt you, Hero."

"This is your only chance. If I find out you're hiding something from me, I won't hold back my wrath."

"Tell me what you think I did. Tell me!" she raises her voice firmly, demanding to know.

But I won't tell her.

If I tell her, I'd have to kill her. I couldn't let her leave my sight. If I did, it would result in my own death when she ran or tried to kill me.

I'm not sure who would win in a fight—her or me. Physically, we are both capable—strong and trained. *But in reality, who would stay emotionally distant enough to kill the other?* We've both let our emotions cloud our judgement when it has come to each other.

Maybe it's time we're honest. Maybe I should tell her what I know before our emotions complicate things further.

I open my mouth, considering speaking, when I hear the front door open and the guys spilling into the entryway.

I close my mouth and step back from Ri.

"Wait...we need to—" she says, but I'm already out the bathroom door and headed toward my bedroom.

I hear her chasing after me, but before she can reach me I hear Hayes shout in relief. "Thank god you're okay, Princess!"

I sneak into my bedroom and close the door just Hayes engulfs her in a hug.

I lean against the door, exhausted and confused and... just so damn tired. I could sleep for days, but I need to go back out. I need to make sure Leighton didn't realize it was us that caused a diversion and stole Ri before I can sleep.

I go to my closet, grab a shirt, and put it on before opening the door to the hallway. I step out just in time to see Ri kiss Caius on the lips.

My heart slams to a stop at the sight. The way she kisses him, the way she seems to slant her head to deepen the kiss, and her groan of pleasure escaping her throat. She's a damn good actress, I'll give her that. She's been playing us all like fools, but I won't be made a fool again.

15

RI

CAIUS PRESSES his lips against mine before I can react. He just lost his father after already losing his sister. He's in a fragile place, and he can't contain showing his feelings toward me. But kissing him after Beckett is like kissing my brother. I'd rather be kissing the man that makes my heart sing.

I push Caius away hard, harder than I probably should for a man who has lost so much and is in mourning. But I have to make myself clear. Just because I like him and I've kissed him in the past doesn't mean I will allow him to kiss me.

"I'm sorry, Caius, but I can't. I care about you a lot, but—"

"But you love him," he answers my sentence.

I narrow my eyes as I stand in front of him. I have only admitted it to myself, not out loud, and definitely not to Beckett. I won't be admitting it to Caius first.

"No, I don't," I say, even though I'm a terrible liar.

Caius just gives me a slim smile, unconvinced. I don't

believe me either, but I won't admit it out loud. It would be foolish to voice such things.

"Don't mention it to anyone else, please," I whisper.

"I won't. Just a bit jealous, that's all."

I touch his forearm in a reassuring manner but don't dare move in for a hug or anything more. I don't want him to get the wrong impression again.

"You should really bow out of the game before you get hurt or killed," I say.

"No."

"But—"

"No, I want to help you. Even if I'm not the one you want, I'd do anything for you. And I can still hold out some hope that the bastard will fuck up with you, and I can swoop in and win your heart. You did call me Charming for a reason after all," Caius winks at me.

I smile, but it's forced. If I did hate Beckett, I wouldn't be able to love Caius, at least not in the way he wants me to.

"You can sleep in my room. The living room couch is a pullout, so I'll sleep there," Caius says.

"Thank you," I say. I'd love to sleep in Beckett's bed, but considering how we just left things, I'm not sure how he feels at the moment.

"I'll just go get a few of my things out of the bedroom and make sure the sheets are clean for you." He brushes past me, and my heart aches for him.

If only, I think with a sigh.

But I have far more important things on my mind.

As soon as Caius leaves me, I rush to Beckett's room. The others have all gone to bed, exhausted as it's almost sunrise now.

I knock on the door and wait.

What was Beckett going to tell me before we were inter-rupted? What does he think I did?

I listen carefully but hear no movement behind the door. I look down at the crack under the door and see the room is in complete darkness.

I try knocking again, louder this time.

Beckett doesn't come to the door. I'm determined to talk to him, though, so I reach for the handle to burst it open. I even push my shoulder against the door to pop it open.

It doesn't budge. He's locked me out.

I consider picking the lock. It's a standard lock and would be easy enough, but then what? He won't talk to me, that much is clear.

"Your bed awaits," Caius says from behind me.

I turn, no longer able to fasten a fake smile on my lips as I head into Caius's room and go to sleep.

————

Once my head hits the pillow, I sleep and sleep and sleep. I didn't realize how exhausted I was until I closed my eyes.

I don't know how many hours or days it has been when I do finally wake up. And when I stand to get out of bed, I know I'm only going to be awake long enough to do one thing—find Beckett and make him talk to me.

I walk out of Caius's bedroom and knock on Beckett's door.

No answer.

No light shines beneath the door.

Nothing.

I pad down the hallway to the kitchen to see if Beckett

is anywhere else in the house. But all I find is Caius sitting at the table with a coffee in hand.

"Good morning, Princess."

"How long did I sleep?"

"Over twenty-four hours."

I nod, but my head throbs at the simple movement, so I quickly stop.

"Do you want a coffee? Food? Anything?"

I move to shake my head but then think better of it. "Just water."

Caius walks to the kitchen and pours me a glass of water. "You should really eat something." He hands me the glass.

"I'm too tired to eat."

Caius frowns.

"Where is everyone else?" I ask, instead of just asking about Beckett. I don't want to hurt Caius more than I have to.

"Out on Retribution Kings business."

I nod. "I'm going back to sleep."

Sleep becomes my routine for the next three days. When I do wake up, I search for Beckett, but he's never here. Occasionally, I drink water or eat a small bite of food, but mostly I sleep.

Beckett is always gone. Gage is also suspiciously absent.

Caius has been making funeral arrangements.

Only Hayes and Lennox have been in the house the last couple of times I've woken up.

"Where is he?" I asked them.

Lennox and Hayes traded looks and gave me some version of the same story. "Sulking. Hiding. Whatever happened between you two is annoying as hell. We can't all be in the same room as him without getting our heads bitten off," Hayes said.

Each time I sighed and went back to bed. It's not like I can do much else. I can't chase after Beckett. I have to stay in the house, so Leighton and Vincent don't know I'm staying here. I don't want to get any of these guys into any more trouble.

After three full days of basically sleeping, I find myself wide awake on the fourth day. Now I can make a plan. I don't know when Beckett returns or leaves, but his bedroom is right next to this one. I can stay up all night and wait for him.

I have to wait until almost five in the morning before I hear his bedroom door open.

I jump up and rush to the door, opening it just in time to see Beckett leaving his bedroom.

We lock eyes, not speaking. Now that we are face to face, I'm not sure what to say. I'm just thankful to see him again. I want answers, but I also just miss him. I miss his musky scent, his longing looks, and his teasing banter. I miss his kisses, his touch, his everything.

The dark stare I get in return tells me he didn't miss me at all. He's looking at me like scum, a blob of gum on the bottom of his shoe that he can't get rid of.

"We need to talk," I say. My words probably don't help the situation. No one likes those words, but they are true. We do need to talk.

"I have nothing to say to you. You're with Caius now. I get it. Play your games with him and hope that he's strong enough to protect you." He glares at me with eyes that I've only seen him give to his enemies.

I catch my breath, confused. *How he could think I'm with Caius?*

"Is that what Caius has been saying? Because it's not—"

"I don't need Caius to tell me what I can see with my own eyes." He grits his teeth. "You're sleeping in his bed, and I saw you kissing him meer seconds after they returned, not more than an hour after I fucked you!"

I narrow my eyes, my jaw clenching. "And did you see that Caius has been sleeping on the couch? Did you see that the second Caius kissed me, I pushed him away? Did the other guys tell you that every time I woke up, I asked where you were?"

He doesn't flinch as the words fly out of my mouth. "Can't you see that you're the only man I want? If it were up to me, I'd chose you and end the games," I say, barely a whisper.

It's the most I've ever shared my feelings with him. Beckett drives me crazy, but in the moments when we are alone, I can see the real him. The him that is loyal to a fault. The hin that would protect me with his life. The him that cares about his friends as if they are family. The man who is dominating and caring. The man who sees the real me and lets me be myself.

There's a beat, then another, before Beckett finally answers. "Go back to sleep, Princess. You owe me, and I'm calling in my prize. Go back to sleep."

I frown as he reaches behind me and opens the door to Caius's bedroom.

"You're insufferable. I have no idea why I like you," I say, storming back into the bedroom mainly to get a gun or knife. I'm determined to force him to talk to me when I freeze dead in my tracks.

My heart seizes, and my breath catches. My lips mumble, trying to get a sound out, but I can barely mutter a syllable, let alone a word. All the hairs on the back of my arms stand up, and a biting coldness spreads through my body.

"B—Beckett," I croak out. It's not loud enough. He's probably stormed out of the apartment by now.

To my shock, the door swings open, and Beckett is immediately at my side, staring at the note on the bed. Someone snuck into this room and left it in the less than five minutes I was outside. He could still be here.

I shiver involuntarily. I already have so many enemies, so many problems, but it's clear I have yet another. And I'm all alone in facing him.

I feel a brush against my fingertips and look down just as Beckett hooks his fingers with mine. Maybe I'm not so alone after all.

16

BECKETT

RI HAS A STALKER. It's part of a pattern, and the guy is skilled. I didn't hear him, even though I was just outside the door, and there are no signs of anyone being here.

I would accuse Ri of leaving the note herself if she weren't white as a ghost, shivering at the sight of the note, her eyes glazed over and lost in painful memories. She knows the man. She knows the stalker.

I doubt she'll tell me who he is; she prefers her secrets. It won't stop me from getting answers, though.

I'm still holding her hand as I step closer to the bed to read the note.

We need to talk. Stop avoiding me. It's urgent. I'll come for you soon. Don't run this time. Be ready.

Ri and I both read the note at the same time, but neither of us picks it up. She sucks in a breath as she reads. He'll be coming for her soon.

Not if I have anything to say about it.

Ri's mine.

Not his.

Mine.

I tighten my grip on Ri's hand, and she looks down at our joined hands. Her nose wrinkles, and her eyes widen in confusion. She doesn't understand why I'm by her side, why I'm holding her hand when I just fought next to her.

"You're mine," I whisper under my breath as I watch goosebumps form on the back of her neck.

"Gage! Everyone get in here!" I yell the next moment, knowing we don't have any time to waste if we are going to find him.

I squeeze Ri flush against my body as Caius is the first to run into the bedroom. She doesn't fight me as I hold her against my chest. And she doesn't look at Caius as he enters.

"What is it? What's wrong?" Caius asks, then stares at Ri. "Princess, are you okay? Are you hurt?"

I ignore his questions. "Where is Gage?"

Caius frowns. "How would I know? Are you going to tell me what's going on? I'm the—"

"You're not the leader anymore; I am. Now, go find Gage."

"I'll find him," Hayes says as soon as he pokes his head in, immediately turning to dash back out.

Lennox arrives next. He doesn't ask any questions, just assesses the situation carefully and then looks at me. "What would you like me to do?"

"Search the premises for any sign of a break-in."

He nods and leaves.

"Go with him, Caius."

Caius looks to Ri like he's waiting for her to say something. She never does. He opens his mouth, about to speak, when I give him a stern look. He doesn't have a choice but to obey my orders.

He turns and follows Lennox out.

Ri reaches her hand out slowly to the bed toward the threatening note, but I pull her back.

"Don't touch it. We might be able to get fingerprints off it."

She nods and looks up at me with big sad eyes. "You're a good leader. Don't let anyone tell you any different."

I don't get any words out to respond to her before Hayes returns with Gage.

It takes Gage less than a second to see the note and realize what it means. "Want me to check the security cameras and see if I can find anyone?"

"Yes. And Hayes can handle sweeping this room trying to find any evidence of who broke in or how," I say.

Hayes nods. "Done, sir."

I wince when he calls me sir.

Ri is dressed in pajama pants with a robe around her body. Her hair is slightly tangled from sleep and having not showered yet for the day.

"Wait here," I tell her.

She doesn't move or protest as I walk to the closet and find her some jeans and a fitted shirt.

I hand them to her. "Change, and then we are leaving."

Her eyebrows raise, as do Hayes's.

"Are you sure about that, boss? Nobody can see Princess, or you'll start a war," Hayes says.

"Nobody will see her."

Ri quickly changes in the bathroom, and then I sneak her out of the apartment the same way I snuck her in.

"The stalker knows I'm here. He could be working for

Vincent or Leighton or any of the other men fighting for me," Ri says solemnly once we are in the car in the garage underground.

"I know."

"Then why did you tell Hayes that nobody will see me?"

"Because it's my job to worry about such things, not his."

I pull the car out of the garage and start driving through the city streets. I have no idea where I'm going or what we are doing. I just know I need to protect her. Her fate is mine to decide. I'm owed that after what she did to Odette.

To my surprise, Ri doesn't ask where we are going. She seems pleased to be out of the apartment and away from the danger. Maybe she feels safer with me as well.

It's a mistake. I'll be the one who ends her life, not saves it. She's always called me 'Hero.' She's about to see how I couldn't be further from that. I'm the opposite of her hero; I'm her villain—and she's mine.

"There's someone following us," Ri says stiffly, looking out the side mirror.

I look in my rearview mirror. There's a flashy red sports car speeding behind us.

I frown. "Whoever it is, they don't care that they are easy to identify."

"It's almost like they want to be caught," Ri says.

"Do you recognize the car or the driver?"

Ri studies the car through the side mirror. "It's hard to make out the driver from here, but I don't recognize the car. None of Vincent's men drive sports cars, not even in their spare time. He would never allow them to stand out and be a magnet for the cops. Maybe one of Leighton's men? Leighton himself?"

I narrow my eyes at the car behind us. I can't make out the man in the driver's seat either.

I make a sharp turn just to see what he does. He follows but at a slower pace. It's like he's not afraid of losing us because he knows exactly where we're going. However, that isn't possible since I don't even know where I'm going.

"Search for a tracker on your body," I say to Ri suddenly.

Her eyes widen. "Shit, you really think...?"

I nod. As much as I don't want to think about it, he was in her room when she was sleeping. He put a tracker on her.

She scrambles, trying to find the device on her body, while I continue to drive.

"We could confront him. Both of us are fully capable of taking on a single man in a fight," Ri says as she searches for the device.

"No, it's like you said. He wants to be caught. It's a trap. Your stalker wants to talk to you. But we aren't going to give him that power."

She stops searching her clothes and just stares at me.

"What?" I ask.

"You said 'we.'" She smiles. "I like that we're in this together."

I roll my eyes. "Just find the device. Then we can ditch him. I'd much rather Gage figure out who he is so we can deal with him on our own terms."

She searches through her pockets, running her hands over the fabric of her clothes. "I can't find anything."

I cringe as the thought hits me. "You changed clothes."

Our gazes hit each other. "No. No!" Ri shivers as she realizes what I'm not saying.

I cringe. "I'm sorry." And I am. No one deserves to be violated like that, not even my greatest enemy.

I turn my eyes back to the road as she starts shimming her pants down. Surprisingly, I don't see much hurt at the violation on her face. It reads more like unstoppable fury. It wouldn't shock me if she killed him before I even figured out who the man is.

I drive slowly, giving her time to find the device, and I keep my eyes off of her, giving her the space she needs to find it—most likely in the most intimate of places. My hand grips the wheel harder, and I find my face turning redder and redder until my nostrils are practically breathing out fire.

"That son of a bitch," Ri curses. I take a chance and turn in her direction.

She's holding a tiny tracking device between her two fingers.

"Stop the car," she says.

"No," I say, even though it's exactly what I want to do. But I won't put her in danger.

"It's not your choice."

"It is actually since I'm the boss now."

"You're not my boss, and you never will be. Now, stop the damn car!"

I sigh and look over at her. She's not thinking clearly, but the anger in her voice is unacceptable. The way her lip wavers and her hands shake—I can't endure her being in this much pain. And I can't think clearly, either. Before I do as she says, I'm barely able to get out a few words. "There's a gun in the glove compartment."

She grabs for it at the same time I stop the car.

We both jump out a second later, each with a gun in our hand aimed at the car. Neither of us shoots. We both want to see the whites of the man's eyes first. This is personal. This man violated Ri in the worse possible way. He doesn't get to get away with this.

His car stops when he sees us with guns.

"Be ready for him to fire at us," I say, knowing this was a bad idea. He has the protection of his car, which might even be bulletproof. We have very few places to hide on this random side street.

Ri keeps stalking forward, and I'm right by her side. I'll let her take the lead. I'll let her be the one who shoots him dead, but I'm going to get at least one painful shot in—most likely to his groin.

For some reason, standing next to Ri like this always feels right. I belong fighting by her side, as her equal. We are equals—equal enemies.

"Why isn't he shooting at us?" Ri asks with a frown.

"I don't know. He may be under instructions not to hurt you from Vincent or Leighton or whoever he works for. It shouldn't stop you from shooting him."

Her lips curl up. "Don't worry; nothing will stop me."

She takes another step forward, and I match her pace. The car doesn't retreat. The man inside doesn't get out. He doesn't fire. He does nothing.

I look through the windshield, but it's too tinted to make out the man inside or what he's doing. If we get much closer, he'll be able to run us over before we can fire a shot. I ache to give a command for us to attack, but I resist. She knows the stakes, same as me. She knows when the time is right to attack and when to play defense. I trust her with this, even if I don't trust her with much beyond being good in a fight.

"Fire!" she yells and starts shooting at the car.

I follow suit.

"Bulletproof," Ri says after shooting a few shots.

We both stop, waiting to see what he's going to do.

There's a loud thud sound that startles us both, but no shots are fired in our direction.

"He's running!" Ri yells and starts chasing after a man fleeing the car.

I chase after her.

He must have rolled out of the back of the car.

I'm usually faster than Ri, but she's got enough anger to fuel her to run twice as fast.

We run down the street and through an alleyway. When I turn into the alleyway, there is no sign of the man, just Ri running through the alley looking lost. She looks in windows, up fire escapes, and at brick walls like he must have moved a wall in order to disappear.

I walk slowly toward her as I pocket my gun, giving her time to accept that he's gone. We'll have to rely on Gage and the others to give us the info we need to find him.

By the time I reach her, she hasn't realized we need to give up our current quest. She's still holding her gun like she's in mortal danger. If I'm not careful, she'll fire that gun in my direction.

"Ri," I say as calmly and carefully as I can.

She doesn't respond or stop. Her eyes are searching wildly as she stands at the base of a fire escape. "Give me a boost."

"Princess," I try again.

She tries to jump to reach the bottom of the ladder, but she can't reach it. There is no way he disappeared up the fire escape. I don't know where he went, but it wasn't up this ladder.

"Fighter..." I touch her shoulder.

She spins.

I brace myself for her to shoot me with the gun or at least hit me with it. Instead, it drops to the ground, and she falls against me.

I wrap my arm around her as she collapses against my chest.

I take a deep breath, taking in the smell of her raven hair. Her scent and face remind me of a river—fresh and strong and flowing with water—strength, not weakness emanating from that liquid, her tears. She smells and feels like she belongs exactly where she is—wrapped around me and held in my arm.

"I'm never going to be free. This is my life. Bad men will always be trying to control me, chasing me, stalking me. My life will never be my own. Whether I wake up the next day will always hang in the balance."

I hold my breath because she's right. This is her life as much as it's my life. And even if I wanted to play hero and save her, there is nothing I could do. She's in too deep, has too many powerful men surrounding her. There is no escape. I should know. I've tried and failed.

"You're the only one who doesn't try to control me." Her eyes are full of tears as she looks up at me.

My brow furrows. "All I've done is try to control you."

She shakes her head with a soft smile on her lips. "We bicker. We fight to be the more dominant one. We tease and taunt, and ridicule. But ultimately, we're equals. We give as much as we get. There is no controlling one another. We're made better and worse by each other. If we were together...that might be the only way either of us gets free."

I don't know what to say to that. I just stare at her

plump lips as a tear rolls down her cheek and then over them. That single tear contains all of her hope for us, but it just disappeared too.

I can't stand for her to lose hope. I need her to fight with me. I need her to hate me, to show me her true colors so I can do what needs to be done for Odette.

But I can't find the words. Instead, I lift her chin and gently kiss the corner of her mouth in the same spot I saw the tear disappear. Maybe my kiss will give her a spark of hope.

The second our lips join, there is a very different kind of spark, though. It makes us both lose all sense of reality, time, and space. The kind that makes me feel like there is more than just sex and a weird agreement to save each other in exchange for debts. It's never felt like this for me with any other woman.

Not Odette.

Not any woman before her.

Only Ri—my fighter.

And then we're kissing. Her arms are around my neck. Mine is around her waist. Our tongues are gliding together, joining like we've kissed a million times and can predict exactly where the other is going to be.

We groan together as a ravenous hunger overwhelms us both. Each kiss is more intense than the last.

"I have no idea how I'm going to give you up," I say through kisses. I meant to keep it to myself, but the thought spilled out of me.

"Then don't."

I growl as she attacks me with everything inside her. Her legs wrap around my waist, and my hand goes her ass. I stumble forward into the wall of the alleyway, pressing her hard against the brick.

"What if I don't have a choice?" *What if you hadn't left me a choice when you ripped out my heart?*

Ri grips my face in her hands. Her eyes dart back and forth over mine as she tries to read my thoughts.

"We always have a choice, even when it seems impossible." She kisses me again, and I become lost in her.

"The only time I truly miss my arm is when I'm with you. I want to be able to touch every part of you, all of you, at once."

She strokes my right arm over the scar that I bear from losing it. "I can understand why you feel that way, but you're more than enough. Your touch is enough. And when I'm with you, I'm not missing anything."

"Fuck me."

"That's what I'm trying to do," she says with a grin.

"You're going to be the death of me."

She reaches for my pants and undoes them as I kiss down her neck.

"And you're going to be the death of me," she moans back.

One of us is right. I just don't know who. Maybe we'll fuck each other to death and end both our suffering right now. I can dream.

She reaches into my pants before I can, again the benefits of having two free hands while I have one still holding her against the wall.

My head falls back at her touch against my cock. She strokes it long and slow like we have all the time in the world. One of her nails teases down the length of me, causing me to swell further in her hand.

"I need to touch you. Hold on." It's all the warning I give before letting go of her legs and undoing her pants. Her legs tighten around my waist, and one of her hands grips my neck tighter as I'm able to pull her pants down just below her ass.

And then I dip my fingers into her folds. She's soaking wet and writhing against my hand as I stroke her.

"You're always so wet for me."

She nibbles on my earlobe. "And you're always so hard for me."

"Maybe I'm just a man who likes to fuck a pretty woman, not just you?"

She bites down hard, hard enough that I'm sure she's left a permanent dent on my ear. "That's a lie."

It is, but I won't tell her that. I prefer her fighting me over loving me.

"I'll go find another woman and show you how true it is."

Her hand on my cock becomes a vice grip. I have no doubt she could rip it off with her bare hand if she wanted to.

"I'd love to see you try. All it would prove is that I'm right and guarantee the loss of your favorite appendage."

I bite the tip of her nose. "It's your favorite appendage too."

Her eyes darken in truth. She releases me.

"Now scream my name and show me how much you love it when I fuck you with it."

I grab her hip and drive my cock inside her in one deep stroke. Her back hits the brick hard, and her nails dig into my back equally as rough. We will both have scars from this one fuck. I just hope it's only on our bodies and not on our hearts.

Her nails dig harder into my skin, holding on for dear life. I feel much the same with every stroke inside her.

Every moment together is fleeting, which makes me want to hold on tighter to her.

For a moment, I think we should run from this world and live happily together. My brother has plenty of yachts to spare. We could hide out on one together. We could be happy. I could be happy.

I know now that I wouldn't have been happy with Odette. The lies would have ended us if she ever loved me to begin with. It's exactly the same reason I would never be happy with Ri, even if her feelings seem more genuine.

I drive harder inside her. Every time I've fucked her, I thought it was the last. This time is no different.

Every thrust tells her how I feel, even if I can't say it with words.

I could have loved you if it weren't for the lies.

I could have loved you if we weren't enemies.

I could have put all of that aside and loved you if you hadn't killed Odette.

I could have...but now I can't.

Her body grips me harder, knowing I'm pulling away, and she won't allow it. We both want to stay like this forever, fucking in the alleyway away from reality. But neither of our bodies can hold on for long; the intensity is too great.

She comes a split second before I do. Her orgasm explodes around us as I bury myself deep inside her again. The feeling is overwhelming. I'm barely able to stay on my feet as stars flood my vision. All I can hope is that I'm dead —that the orgasm was too much for my body to bear, and I'm now dead. Then I won't have to worry about anything anymore. Then I could die happy.

But Ri strokes my cheek, and I know I'm not dead. I'm

just in my own personal hell. A hell that is going to end with me turning into the devil.

Her eyes are filled to the brim with love. I can see it even though she doesn't say it. I refuse to search my own heart for how I feel. I'm done listening to the bastard; it's betrayed me too many times already.

Whatever she thinks she's feeling, it can't be real love. If she loved me, she wouldn't have killed Odette. She could have flirted with me. She could have tried to show me that she was better for me than Odette. And when I learned the truth about Odette, maybe I would have come running to Ri.

Now it's too late.

I step back and gently put her back on her feet. We both awkwardly readjust our clothes.

Ri opens her mouth; I'm sure to say something sappy or caring.

I don't give her a chance. "The next game starts tomorrow. The guys should have figured out who your stalker is by now. We need to get back and make a plan for both."

Then I start walking back to the car, away from Ri, like I don't give a damn about her. She's just a good fuck; that's all she is.

At least, that's what I keep trying to convince myself.

17

RI

EVERY TIME BECKETT FUCKS ME, it feels like he's telling me goodbye. Every. Damn. Time.

And every time I fuck him, I fall more in love with him. I can't explain it. It's like I know him, more than what he shows, more than what he pretends to be. Like I've known him my entire life. Like we are two lost souls who find solace in each other when we're together.

When we are fucking, it's the only time Beckett lets himself be himself. It's the only time he lets himself feel for me.

Now that it's over, he'll go back to hating me and pretending I mean nothing to him.

Sure enough, that's exactly what he does as he stomps back to the car without looking back.

I can't wipe the grin off my face, though, not after that orgasm. Not after it got rid of any thoughts of the violation I felt just a few minutes earlier.

I jog to catch up to Beckett as he turns toward the street the car is parked on. He stops suddenly, and my gaze turns to where he's looking.

The stalker's car is gone. That must have been how he escaped while we were fucking.

Neither of us speaks about it. There is nothing to say. We climb into the car in silence, and Beckett starts driving. Soon, we're parked again at Caius's place.

This time when we get there, we climb up the stairs on our own. Beckett doesn't carry me, and I don't make a game out of it.

"Did you identify him?" Beckett asks the others as soon as we enter Caius's apartment.

I follow behind and find the guys all sitting on their laptops at the kitchen table.

"No, we haven't figured out who he is," Lennox says.

Beckett ignores him and looks right at Gage like they are trying to communicate without words.

"Sit down, Princess. You must be starving. I'll make you something," Hayes says, breaking the tension.

He pulls out his chair for me, and I take a seat. Caius reaches across the table and squeezes my hand. "Don't worry; we'll find him and make sure he doesn't threaten you again."

I squeeze his hand back and then release it. "I know, thank you."

Beckett doesn't sit. He just paces while Hayes cooks some food in the kitchen.

A few minutes later, Hayes has a gourmet sandwich sitting in front of me and a cup of coffee. He offers one to Beckett, but he declines.

"Do you have any idea who it was, Princess? One of your father's men? He would have to be very skilled to be able to sneak in and out without anyone noticing," Gage asks me.

I can feel Beckett's stare on me like he thinks I know

who it is, and I'm purposefully sending his team on a wild goose chase. I don't look in his direction. I keep my eyes on Gage, who seems equally accusing, while the others seem completely oblivious.

"Vincent has plenty of men capable of doing what the stalker did. I'm sure Leighton does, as does every other man competing in Vincent's game," I say.

"Can you think of anyone specifically?" Gage asks, not giving up.

"I can make you a list of all of Vincent's men who I think would be capable, but I honestly have no idea why he would send a man to stalk and threaten me. If Vincent wanted me to do something, all he'd have to do is summon me, and I'd do it." I don't have a choice if I want to keep Beckett alive.

For some reason, my comment makes Beckett's stare darken. I can't resist looking at him this time. He glares at me like he wants to murder me when less than an hour ago he was fucking me with love.

I sigh and take a bite of my sandwich. I don't care what Beckett thinks anymore. I have bigger things to worry about at the moment, like the fact that I have a new enemy capable of avoiding my guys.

"What about tomorrow? What are we going to do about getting Princess to the games without Corsi finding out we've had her this whole time?" Lennox asks.

"Let him know that we've had her. I'm not afraid of Corsi," Caius says.

"No, I'm not going to risk your lives. I'll show up alone and tell Vincent that after Leighton tried to hurt me, I fought my way out and have been hiding out until the game," I say.

"I don't think you need to worry about protecting us,

Princess. Every man here has had his dick in you. If Corsi finds that out, we're all dead. Hiding you for a few days doesn't seem like it will matter in comparison," Hayes teases, putting his hand on my shoulder.

I swat his hand away but don't blush. I don't care if I've fucked all of them.

"Well, I don't want any of you taking any further risks on my behalf."

Beckett chuckles. "Too late for that, Princess."

I glare at him for calling me Princess.

I take another bite of my sandwich and then pick up my coffee as I stand. "I'm going to go take a shower. Let me know if you find anything on my stalker."

Then I head to the bathroom without another word. I close the bathroom door and sink to the floor as dark memories flood my head. Of course, I know who it was—Kek, my dark nightmare. Neither I nor Vincent has ever been able to protect me from him. These guys don't stand a chance. I need to find a way to meet him before people start turning up dead.

I step out of the shower and wrap a towel around my waist before I feel Beckett's angry presence. My breath catches as I slowly turn around to face him. His eyes are laser-focused on mine, ignoring my bare chest and legs. Like if he looks down further, he'll be tempted by my body and not say what he came here to say. Like I'll somehow manipulate him.

I lick my lips to test my theory. His eyes drop just the slightest, and his lips tighten into a thin slit. The muscles in his jaw grow taunt.

"I know what you're hiding," he says.

I raise an eyebrow. "Do you? Because it seems like you're the one hiding secrets."

His eyes finally drop, unable to help himself. His finger traces down my arm, over the still healing wound on my bicep. He stops and turns, about to walk away.

I reach out my hand and touch his bare arm, down to the scar on the end before my hand finds nothing but air in a similar way that he touched me.

"We both have secrets. We both have our reasons for keeping them secret. It shouldn't stop us from enjoying each other every second we get. It shouldn't stop us from fighting for a future together."

He turns and frowns at me. "There is no future together."

I shrug. "Probably not, but we should still fight for one. I'm not going to pretend that I'd be happy with any man but you. And you'll never find another woman you're more fascinated with than me."

Beckett strokes the ends of my wet hair. "I'm not sure I can pretend when there are too many lies between us."

"The lies don't involve one another. We don't lie to each other or keep secrets because we don't trust each other. We keep secrets because they are our burdens to bear. Sharing our secrets would ruin everything."

He leans in close, too close. "Why? Because your secret would prove that you aren't an innocent princess?"

I frown. "You already know I'm not an innocent princess, just as I know you aren't a chivalrous hero. It doesn't change anything. Our secrets aren't who we really are. This life isn't who we really are. We're both trapped, doing whatever it takes to survive in our unending prison."

His thumb strokes my jaw. "I want to know your secrets. I want to know everything. You want to talk about a future, about feelings. I've been burned too many times,

Princess, to open myself up to feel until I know every secret you're hiding."

I swallow hard. I should tell him the truth, everything I know, but I don't want to put Beckett in any more danger. If Kek knows I'm here, he'll already see Beckett as a threat. I can't tell Beckett anything. I need to protect him, keep him safe. If I can't have Beckett, the least I can do is keep him alive.

I need to give him up and get him to quit the game—him and Caius both. They need to bow out gracefully. That's the only way to ensure they survive, *but how do I convince them?*

Beckett reads the emotions all over my face. He sees the moment I realize I can't tell him anything—the disappointment on his own face is devastating. I want nothing but to wipe that disappointment off his face. I want nothing more than to tell him everything, for us to fall madly in love, fight all the odds together and win, then live our happily ever after together.

It doesn't matter what I want, though—I can't have it. All I can do is save the people that I love.

"Our deal ends today," I say.

Beckett cocks his head like he doesn't understand me.

"I don't want you to save me anymore. From now on, we're each on our own." I don't know how I'm going to convince him to give up the game when he thinks my father killed Odette. He thinks the only way to get retribution is to win the game and then take me far away from my father.

I'll find a different way. First, I need him to stop putting his life in danger for me.

His eyes flick back and forth over mine as he tries to

figure out what I'm not telling him. My heart is breaking, giving him up. He's the only thing I've ever wanted for myself.

"Why?" he asks, his voice deep.

"I never wanted or needed a hero. It felt good to have one for a bit, and I'm thankful to you. But I'm ready to face whatever comes by myself."

I brush past him to where my clothes lay on the sink counter. "And if you're smart, you'll pull out of the game."

He raises a brow. "I thought you liked me? I thought you wanted me to win? I thought I was your best chance at getting what you wanted?"

I make my face blank, void of emotion where Beckett is concerned. "I did like you, but I like myself more. I'm going to win. If I have to take you down with the rest of them, then so be it. You've been a good friend and a great fuck, but I won't let any man have power over me, not anymore. Take Caius and get out before you both end up dead."

Beckett walks to me. He doesn't touch me, but he seems to want to. He leans in until his hot lips are against my ear. "I don't know what game you're playing at, Princess, but I'm not going anywhere. I'll try to convince Caius to quit. He should have a long time ago, but you won't get rid of me so easily. I know what you're up to, and I can play the game better than you. You're a good opponent, but I never lose. And don't worry, I'm done playing hero."

And then Beckett leaves me alone in the bathroom.

The rest of the day, I don't see him. The guys mill about discussing options for who my stalker could be and what he could want. They discuss what the game could be tomorrow. They never let me out of their sight, and Beckett is nowhere to be found.

By ten o'clock, I'm exhausted and decide to head to bed. After changing and brushing my teeth, I walk back into Caius's bedroom that I have commandeered as my own to find Gage sitting on the chair in the corner on his laptop. Hayes and Lennox are making makeshift cots on the floor. Caius is leaning against the doorway, drinking whiskey.

None of them really surprise me. They all fucked me to protect me, knowing it could be the last thing they did. But what surprises me is the man adjusting the covers on the bed.

"Get in the bed, Princess," Beckett says in his deep, commanding voice.

I fold my arms over my chest. "I think this is a little unnecessary. No one is going to break in while I sleep."

"Can't be too careful," Hayes says with a smile.

"Lennox, I don't really think you need to sleep here too."

"Just following orders," Lennox says, lying down on the bed of comforters and pillows he's arranged for himself on the floor on my side of the bed. He winks at me, and I know that it's not just about orders. He cares; deep down, he cares.

I frown as I look around at the room of men who could be dead tomorrow. And if they survive tomorrow, they might be gone the next day or the day after. Caring for me is a death sentence. I have to make them all stop caring.

"Don't," Beckett says, staring at me with disdain.

"What?"

"I know what you're thinking. Don't. It will make everything worse."

I frown.

"Get your smart ass to bed and stop acting you like you know what's best," Beckett says.

"I do know what's best," I reply.

He shakes his head as I climb into bed. As I do, he whispers, "If you did, you'd trust me with your secrets."

Shivers rattle through me as he covers me with the comforter.

Caius walks toward the bed out of the corner of my eye when Beckett says, "You're on first shift, Caius. Wake Hayes, and he'll take the second shift. Then Lennox will take third."

"What about Gage?" Caius asks.

"I'm looking for the damn stalker, so we don't have to do this every night. I'll work as much as I can and then sleep and do it all over again," Gage grumbles.

Caius sighs and storms out.

"He doesn't like giving up control. It's harder than he thought it would be," Hayes says.

"No shit," Beckett says before getting under the covers next to me.

My eyes widen in shock, and my mouth falls open.

Beckett smirks at my reaction. "What? Can't handle sleeping next to me, Princess?"

"Nothing wrong with it; just know that I'm a kicker."

"A kicker?"

I knee him in the groin.

He moans dramatically, rolling away from me.

I grin.

Lennox and Hayes snicker. Even Gage grins from behind his computer.

I try to play the ice princess—aloof and unaffected by Beckett being in my bed. I try to pretend I hate him, that I don't want him. But I'm going to have to up my acting skills if I want to save his life. Everyone's life in this room hangs in the balance, and I'm the only one who can keep us all alive.

18

BECKETT

Rɪ's ɢᴏɴᴇ.

I can feel it before I even open my eyes. She's gone.

The question is, who took her?

Or did she sneak out on her own?

Did she leave willingly?

And how the hell did she sneak out or get taken without any of us waking up?

I open my eyes, confirming the empty spot on the bed. I sit up quickly, hoping no one is hurt or missing.

As I scan the room, I see Caius and Hayes sleeping on the floor. Gage is asleep in the chair, and I presume Lennox is out on patrol.

She could be in the bathroom or kitchen with Lennox.

I jump up and run to the bathroom, but it's empty.

When I make it back to the bedroom, the guys begin to stir.

"What's going on?" Caius asks, probably noticing the way my hand is balled into a fist and my jaw is clamped tight.

I don't answer him. I storm out of the bedroom. "Lennox!"

He comes running down the hallway but stops dead when he sees me.

"Where is Ri?" I bark.

He looks at me like I'm crazy. "In the bedroom, asleep."

"No, she's not in the bedroom."

He frowns. "I don't understand...someone has been awake all night. How could someone have taken her without waking everyone up? Are you sure she's not somewhere in the condo?"

The rest of the guys are now standing around, watching us with shock on their faces.

Gage is the only one who looks at me, and I know he's thinking the same thing I am. The only way this could have happened is if Ri was in on it. Neither of us speaks our thoughts out loud.

"It had to be the same guy who left the note. Who else is capable of sneaking in and out unnoticed?" Hayes asks.

Lennox and Caius mumble their agreement. I keep silent.

"What should we do? Where do we start looking for her?" Caius asks.

My phone buzzes, and I pull it out—a message from Corsi.

"Is it her? Is she alive?" Hayes asks, worry in his voice.

"It's Corsi. The game starts at midnight, and we are to bring our crews," I say, looking at the guys. It was never my intention to put their lives in danger.

"If the stalker took Ri, I don't think he'll hurt her. I still believe he may be working for Corsi. We keep trying to track down the stalker. That will give us the best lead to Ri," I say.

I take a deep breath. "But I don't want anyone exhausted for tonight. We don't know what the game is or how challenging it is. None of you have to come tonight if you don't want to. The game will inevitably be dangerous, and I won't ask you to risk your life lightly. It will be your choice."

Everyone stares back at me like I've lost my mind. "We're all coming," says Caius.

———

It's midnight on the dot when we arrive at the game's location in an abandoned building. We've dressed all in black and geared up for battle.

"Everyone ready? You can still back out," I say as we sit in the SUV, checking our weapons one last time before we enter what will surely be a life or death battle. I don't know how many men survived the last game, but I saw the carnage. I saw men bleeding to death, and most that survived had serious injuries. Tonight, I can't guarantee everyone's safety.

"We're all coming. Retribution Kings stick together. Besides, we need to make sure Ri is okay," Hayes says.

I scan everyone else, and they each seem just as determined as Hayes. Even Gage, who knows more of the truth than anyone else.

"Keep your wits about you. And follow my lead," I say as I get out.

"That's what being the leader means. We follow your lead," Lennox teases. Everyone chuckles, breaking the tension.

We walk up to the large building. The exterior looks like it hasn't been occupied for at least a decade. Paint is chipping, the windows are broken, and the door is barely blocking the doorway.

We walk through the broken door and into the warehouse. It's almost pitch black as we walk, water dripping down on our heads from broken pipes and the cracked ceiling.

Far off voices are the only clues of other people in the warehouse besides ourselves. We continue walking toward the voices, through a door where a lone light shines. The room is illuminated, and everyone else comes into view.

Men are gathered in groups around the room, but that's not what has drawn all of our attention.

It's Ri—no, Rialta Corsi. That's who she is.

Manipulative.

Cunning.

Scheming.

Heartless.

Rialta Corsi—the mafia princess.

She's standing in a group of men who are laughing at something she said. They're hanging onto her every word as she grips their arms and flirts with each bat of her eyelashes. She's dressed in all black like everyone else here, but her makeup is done up. Her long hair is flowing, and her tight clothes are meant for easy movement as much as they are for seducing every man here.

Hayes stops dead. "Ri's safe and—"

"And happy to play her part," I finish his sentence.

He frowns as he looks at me. "I don't understand. Did one of those men kidnap her?"

I doubt it, but I don't say a word.

I notice Leighton eyeing the crew she's with suspiciously like he's planning their deaths in his head.

Ri finally notices us staring at her. I watch as her eyes

cut in my direction with a deep scowl on her face. She's not happy we're here, or at least that's the ruse she's currently playing.

I don't understand her game. I don't understand if she wants me for herself or she wants me dead, but I'm beginning to grow tired of playing the game.

Corsi steps forward and starts talking, but I'm barely listening. All I can do is stare at Ri, trying to read what she's not saying, what she could possibly be planning.

Gage steps next to me. "What do you want to do?"

I know what he means. *Are we going to keep pretending we don't know it was Ri who is responsible for Odette's death while my days as leader of the Retribution Kings tick away? Am I just going to run out the clock and let the Kings kill me instead of doing what has to be done?*

I stare at Ri one last time, silently commanding her to confess from across the room. Explain how she could kill the love of my life. Explain any of her dozens of confusing actions. Of course, she doesn't. She couldn't even if she wanted to.

I'm no longer interested in risking our lives playing this game. I don't want to win Rialta. I don't want to marry her to get back at her father for what he's done. There is only one punishment worthy of what has happened, and the sooner I get it over with, the better.

"We are going to end this tonight. We win her. We take her. Then she'll face judgment in front of the Retribution Kings."

19

RI

A RUSH of hot lust washes over me, a chill brushes against my spine, and my blood blazes like a wildfire through my body. I don't have to look away from Ryker to know that Beckett is here.

The pull to him is deep and torturous to resist, but somehow I resist it for several minutes. I don't want Beckett thinking I care about him. I need him to quit. I need him and the others safe. It's the only thing I can do for them.

Sneaking out in the middle of the night was incredibly hard. Not just logistically, but leaving Beckett lying in bed, giving him no explanation for my departure, my heart broke. It broke, leaving all of them.

Ryker is the leader of the Devil Crew. He's a wretched man, merciless and cruel—the last man I would ever want to marry. I waited outside until I saw him arrive, went in with him, and flirted my way into his inner circle.

When Leighton arrived, I knew he'd blame Ryker for my kidnapping. Pitting two of my worst enemies against each other is the only way I could think of to save Beckett from suspicion.

I'm not sure if Vincent believes my ruse, but from the way Leighton has been glaring at Ryker, it seems to have at least convinced Leighton.

Finally, I let myself glance at Beckett. Most people that look at him would only see a bored, reserved man. But when I look at him, I see the bulging vein on his neck, his dilated eyes as he looks at me, and the slight tension in his hand. He's beyond angry that I left in the middle of the night without a word.

Good, maybe this will start him down a path where he finally gives me up. I just need to find a reason for him to quit these games—something so dangerous it's not worth continuing to risk his team's lives.

Maybe even tonight, I can get him to bow out if I can influence the game and make it seem more dangerous for Beckett's team without actually hurting any of them. Beckett won't leave for himself, but he might pull out if it risks Hayes, Lennox, Gage, or Caius.

Vincent steps into the center of the room and starts explaining the new game, but it's not that hard to follow. It's a drug run. The goal is to move drugs from one location to another without getting killed or caught by the police—simple enough.

There are no rules, so each team of men is a threat to the others. You can shoot, injure, or kill anyone on the other teams to try and stop them.

The winner is the first one to complete the run. Anyone who fails to complete the run is dismissed from the game.

People start mumbling plans to their as Vincent is still speaking.

"Silence!" Vincent says when the murmurs get too loud. The room immediately falls quiet, and he continues.

"I'd like to add one small challenge to the game Xavier has chosen for us. This game is meant to challenge your leadership skills as well as the men you have selected with your trust. It will truly test if you have good skills when it comes to selecting men, so I would like to incapacitate the leaders to some extent," he says.

Incapacitate? What does that mean? Vincent looks at me with cold eyes. His eyes tell me this is the round he wants me to lose, but I just cock a brow feigning confusion. If he doesn't officially give me a rule or bargain, then I can't disobey him.

"The leaders will be injected with a drug of my choosing. You will have a few minutes after the injection before the effects take over to make a plan with your team. But after the drug takes over, your facilities with be greatly reduced."

Drugged.

Vincent is going to drug us.

Jesus Christ.

I'm going to be drugged. I don't have a team to help me, no one to rely on. And I'll be surrounded by a hundred men who will be looking to attack me. To hurt me. To make me theirs.

Not to mention every time I've been drugged, my memory gets fuzzy. I lose whole sections of time of my life.

I look at Vincent, suspecting that he added this part of the game because he knew how I'd feel about it. But when Vincent stares back at me, there's no emotion in his eyes, no gleam of satisfaction.

I notice Beckett staring at me out of the corner of my

eye, probably trying to figure out if I'm going to accept the game or not. But I can't think of him right now.

"You're welcome to some of my men, Princess," Ryker says as he puts his hand on my shoulder.

I fight the urge to throw his hand off because I'm going to need the help to survive and to make my plan work.

"Thank you, Ryker. I really appreciate it."

"Calvin, Jace—assist Princess here with whatever she needs," Ryker snaps at two of his closest men. "They're some of my best men, but I'd appreciate it if you don't beat me. I'd like to spend the week with you."

Ryker leaves us alone, and I take in my new teammates —men I'm going to have to depend on if I want to survive tonight unharmed.

I'm so screwed.

"I'm Calvin," the first man with dirty blonde hair and tattooed arms says, holding his hand out to me.

I shake it tentatively.

"And I'm Jace," the taller man with much darker hair says.

"I'm Ri."

"We know," Calvin says with a smile.

"I'm not sure this is the best idea. I—"

"Ryker isn't a bad guy as much as you think he is. I know you're setting him up for Leighton to think Ryker took you. I don't know why you're framing him, but he knows what he's doing. You can trust him," Jace explains.

"How can I trust any man playing a game to marry me? Who will force me to carry his children? Who steals, sells drugs, and murders for a living?"

Jace looks to Ryker. "Yes, Ryker is all those things. But he's the only man here who offered you some of his men to help you. And if he wins, he's the only man who will give you a choice. He only entered the game to stave off the coming gang war. He's doing this to protect our families and us."

I frown, not sure what to do with any of the information.

"You don't have to trust us, but trust that your father will kill us if we let you die, and I'd really rather live. I have two young kids," Jace says, pulling a picture from his wallet of what looks to be a three-year-old boy and a young baby girl with his dark curly hair.

I look him in the eyes and know he's telling the truth. He won't let any harm come to me.

I look to Calvin. "He's my best friend, and I'm godfather to his kids. If he dies, then I become a father, and I'm not ready for that shit."

I chuckle. "Fine, I accept that we are on the same side."

A man walks around distributing bags of drugs to each team with an address.

"So, what's the plan, boss?" Calvin asks, looking at me, as does Jace.

I hold out the address for them to see. "We get here as fast as possible and don't get killed in the process. We stay away from Leighton but shoot to kill if he attacks. And..." I hesitate, trying to decide what to do about Beckett.

"What do you want us to do about Beckett?" Jace asks.

I raise my eyebrow. "Why would you ask about Beckett?"

"He's the strongest here, the biggest threat. And you seem to have a fascination with him."

I frown. "Make it hard for him and his team, but don't kill any of them."

"So I was right? You do have feelings for him?"

"No, I just owe him a debt," I say sternly, pretending

that I don't feel anything for Beckett. In reality, I feel every-thing, every damn emotion under the rainbow.

Then I notice one of Vincent's men going around and beginning the injections. My heart thumps wildly in my chest as I think about what will happen when it's my turn.

"Are you armed?" Jace asks, drawing my attention back to him.

I nod.

"And you can shoot?"

"I can hold my own. But once the drugs hit me..."

Calvin squeezes my shoulder. "We've got you. Once the drugs hit, we'll carry you the entire way and make sure no one hurts you."

"Thank you." His words seem genuine, but I'm not sure I trust these guys fully. *Are they kind and sweet, doing this out of the generosity of their hearts, or do they have another motive?*

I look around the room. Most groups have several men; some even have a dozen. I only have two. The odds are against us.

I spot Geno, one of Vincent's men, moving closer to me with the injection. My time is running out to discuss everything with these two strangers on whom I'm going to depend.

I think about Jace's two little kids. I spot the wedding ring on Calvin's finger. They have a family relying on them.

"Don't risk your life for me. Protect me if you can, but don't die for me."

Calvin and Jace both scowl. "I don't think either of us can promise that."

"You have to, or I won't accept your help. Don't die protecting me."

"And if we let you die, we're dead no matter what," Calvin says.

"No, Vincent won't hold it against you. You're asking me to trust you, so trust me too. Vincent won't harm you."

They exchange glances and even look back at Ryker before they both finally nod at me.

"What do you want us to do about Ryker?" Jace asks.

"What do you mean?"

"If we should encounter him or his men, do we fight? Defend? Team up?"

I think for a moment as Geno is now injecting Ryker.

I take a deep breath. "Team up if you think he'll help. If not, then defend, but I don't want you to have to choose between him and me. Do what you must."

Jace narrows his eyes. "Are you alright? You're shaking."

I nod. "I just don't have the best reaction to drugs, and I don't like giving up control."

My hands fidget with the hem of my shirt, rolling it between my thumb and forefinger nervously.

Calvin tries to hold my hand, but I don't let him. They might be able to protect me physically, but they won't be able to help me psychologically once the drugs hit my system. Once that happens, I could forget everything. I could forget Beckett, my plan to keep him safe, even that I love him.

That is what devastates me most—I might forget the only man I've ever loved.

Geno walks toward me. He pulls a syringe out of his bag and fills it from a vial. My guess is heroin or a heavy tranquilizer that he's about to inject into my arm. I've been drugged so many times that my body can't handle anything stronger than alcohol anymore.

"Ready, Rialta?" Geno asks.

I nod. At the last second, I let my gauze land on Beckett across the room as I hold my arm out for Geno to find a vein. I feel the sharp stab of the needle as it enters a vein.

I don't react. I don't wince in pain. I don't shake. I just stare at Beckett, not to show him emotion or that I care, but just because this may be the last time that I can look at him and remember how I feel, remember him.

I feel the warmth of the drugs flowing through my veins. I force myself to close my eyes and lock Beckett out. It's for the best if I forget him. It will make giving him up so much easier.

20

BECKETT

I WATCH the needle slide into Ri's arm. I can't look away. I want to run to her, put a stop to it. I don't, though. I dig my feet into the ground and root myself to the floor.

Gage tries to say something to me, but I barely look his way. All I see is Ri.

And then she looks at me.

I expect to see anger, pain, fear.

Instead, she looks through me like she's taking in every line on my face, every freckle, every scar. I return the favor, memorizing everything about her.

Just as suddenly, she squeezes her eyes shut as the needle leaves her skin, and she's gone to me. She doesn't look at me again. She turns and faces the two men she's now teamed up with, men that belong to Ryker.

"Everyone ready?" I ask, knowing I'm about to have a drug injected into my body and could lose consciousness or my ability to think at any moment.

"We're ready," Hayes says.

Hayes and Lennox are in charge of keeping Caius safe, while Gage is in charge of keeping me safe. We will all work together as one big team unless we have to split up since Caius and I received the same address with our respective drug packages.

The man walks over with his bag of drugs. "Arm, please."

I hold out my arm and watch as he injects the needle. The warm-hot liquid spreads through my body. I've never done drugs, so I have no idea what to expect or how my body will respond to whatever he just injected, but I suspect it won't be pleasant.

When he finishes with me, he does the same to Caius.

"You okay?" I ask Caius when the man leaves.

He nods. He's been very quiet through all of this. I don't know how he feels about being injected with an unknown drug, but he also wouldn't quit when I asked him to. I don't love the guy, but I don't want to see him killed. I don't know how to get him to quit the game without him ending up dead.

Gage grabs my arm. "Let's go; with any luck, you'll still be with it long enough for us to see how this is going to play out."

I follow Gage, but he doesn't let go of my arm. I think he's too worried about me immediately going into a haze.

We make it to the car we all rode here together in. Caius climbs into the third row with Lennox. I climb into the second row, and Hayes and Gage ride in the front.

"Feel anything yet?" I ask Caius.

"No, you?"

"Nothing."

"Maybe they didn't actually inject you with anything except saline. Maybe it's all to fuck with your head. I can't imagine that Corsi would actually drug his own daughter," Hayes says.

"Then you don't know Corsi very well." I run my hand through my hair, my body feeling warm, possibly feverish, but I don't tell them that. It could be all in my head, or it could be real. Either way, there is nothing we can do about it now.

"Just drive. The faster we get there and get this over with, the faster you can throw Caius and me in a bed to sleep it off," I say.

"Preferably not together," Caius jokes.

I stare out into the darkness as Hayes drives. I don't know where Ri went or if the drugs started to take effect for her already. I just hope she remembers me when she wakes up. I hope that when Gage and I's plan works, she will remember what she did when I extract my retribution.

We drive for over an hour toward the location where we are supposed to deliver our suitcases filled with drugs. We don't see any other teams on the way, and we aren't attacked. There doesn't appear to be any danger as we park the car at the edge of the woods, but that means nothing.

"Good?" I ask Caius before I pull out my gun.

"Good," he responds like he has a dozen times over the last hour.

We all step out of the car, carefully shutting our doors, so they don't make a sound.

"It's so strange. It's way too easy," Lennox says quietly, barely above a whisper.

We all nod our agreement, and I take the first step into the trees. The house we are supposed to drop the drugs off at is about three miles into the center of this wilderness. There are no roads, so we will have to walk.

It's rained recently, so we're forced to trek through

thick mud. It's going to make the hike take longer than it should, but I'd rather deal with the mud than bullets flying by my head.

Lennox leads the way as we walk silently, each of us with a gun in hand, ready for an attack that may not ever come. After twenty minutes of walking, it seems that no danger will come. This is more or less a silly race and nothing more.

Suddenly, there's a crack of a branch overhead. I jump behind the trunk of a tree, crouching down and staring up at the sky. My blood is pumping through me a million miles an hour as I try to make out the attacker through the shadows.

A large bird spreads its wings and takes to the sky, diving out of a tree, causing another crack in the branch above.

I let out a deep breath. "It's just a bird."

And then a bullet whizzes by my head.

Chaos breaks out all around. The quiet quickly turns to loud shouting and the sound of gunfire. I can't even tell which direction the fire is coming from.

I try to open my mouth to shout out orders, but my voice cracks, and nothing comes out.

I see a man cross in front of me. I can't make out exactly who he is, but I know it's not any of my men.

I move to raise my arm to fire at him, but I can't move my arm. I can't move anything. I can barely see a foot in front of me from a haze coating my eyes. Moving my arm through the air feels like moving it through mud. I can move it, but just barely, and it takes all of my effort and concentration to do so.

I'm slowly being paralyzed by the drugs. It doesn't seem to have affected my brain yet, just my body. *But what can I do with any strategy I come up with if I can't use my body to carry it out?*

I search through the darkness, trying to find Gage or Lennox or Hayes, even Caius. I can't find any of them. I see only shadows running through the woods.

The world starts spinning, and I lean my head back against the tree trunk, closing my eyes briefly. I squeeze my forehead with my hand to try to stop my headache. When I open my eyes, the dizziness is worse.

We are still a good mile or two away from the house. It will take me all night if I try to walk now, but that's my only option. I need to start walking and hope that Gage or one of my other men find me. I'll have to stay low to the ground to keep from being seen since I'm in no condition to fight.

I start army crawling on the ground, slinking from behind the tree trunk to behind a bush. It takes so much energy out of me that I realize I can't do this for miles.

I'm sweating profusely, my hand and legs shaky, and I can barely make out what's in front of me. I'm not sure how I'm going to survive.

And then I see her.

Ri.

She's running fast, faster than I've ever seen her run. She's gripping a gun in her hand, and she doesn't look behind her. She doesn't appear impacted by the drugs in her system, at least not yet.

I try to call out to her, to offer my help, but I can't help her. I'm a paralyzed fool who can't speak, let alone fight. She's on her own.

My gaze drifts behind her, and I see the man she's running from—her stalker.

I frown.

Is he one of the men fighting to marry her?

If so, how did we not realize who he was earlier?

She runs into a hard chest, coming to a quick stop. My heart sinks because I want to be the one to help her, but I know she's in safe hands as much as it annoys me.

I watch her in his arms. I watch him hold onto her, protecting her when I can't.

She smiles at him when she should be smiling at me.

She holds onto him when she should be holding onto me.

He leans in and whispers something in her ear, and her demeanor instantly changes.

Her eyes glaze over as if in a trance. He releases her, and instead of running, she turns to face the man she fears more than anything.

I don't know what happened. I don't know what he said to her that caused such a swift change, but she turns to fight.

She's one of the best fighters I know, but with the drugs coursing through her system, she shouldn't fight—not right now. She should run and hide and find the two men who are supposedly on her side. These drugs could rob her of control of her abilities at any second.

I try shouting.

I try to stand.

I try to do anything to get her attention. But I'm trapped in my own body, unable to move, unable to help her.

I hold my breath as I watch. This is my nightmare—being so close to someone I love who is hurting and not being able to do anything about it.

Love.

Fuck.

I love her.

I hate her, and I love her.

I wasn't sure it was possible to love someone you hate, but there it is—the truth.

I love Ri.

I'm still pissed at her and want her to pay for the sins she's committed, but I love her in equal measure.

I love how independent she is, how strong. I love her fighting spirit. I love that she puts me in my place. I love that she's my equal in every way.

I just don't know whose side she's on. *Is she my enemy or my ally?*

Should I love her or tell my heart to stop the bleeding? Every other time I've fallen for a woman, I've fallen for the wrong one.

All I know is I don't want her to die, not now, not like this.

The man gets closer to her, holding his gun casually in his hand. She doesn't move. She stands there, ready for a fight.

Run!

I open my mouth and beg my voice to work, but it doesn't.

Please, Fighter, run!

She doesn't run. She holds her ground.

The man gets closer and closer until she can easily see him.

Shoot him!

She doesn't raise her gun, probably wanting to disarm and kill him in a much more personal way. She shouldn't risk it, though. Everyone is preoccupied with the battle that has broken out. No one is around to protect her.

Any second now, the drugs will engulf her, and she'll

be trapped just like me. I'm surprised it hasn't already affected her. Her system must have a higher tolerance to the drugs after being injected multiple times before.

I wait for her to attack, to make her move. But by the time she launches herself at him, it's too late.

He gets her in a hold. Her arms are pinned behind her back as he whispers something into her ear. I can't tell if he has a gun or knife against her throat.

I try with everything in me to yell for help, but only a whisper comes out.

I can't help her.

I can't save her.

I'm destined to watch another woman I love be taken from me or killed in front of my own eyes.

My heart bursts at the thought, but I don't give up. I can't. Any moment the drugs could wear off enough so I could help her.

Fight him. You're strong enough. You can win.

She wiggles a little in his grasp, but only barely.

Why isn't she fighting harder?

Did the drugs hit her? Is she just as helpless as I am?

I don't blink. I can't tear my eyes from her, not even for that split second. So much emotion and adrenaline are rushing through me; I must be able to break through the hold of the drugs soon.

The man whispers something into Ri's ear, and she goes lax.

I narrow my eyes, confused at what I'm seeing.

The man releases her and is gone as fast as he came.

My heart beats again when I see Ri still standing and seemingly unhurt. I want to run to her, put my arm around her, and get her the hell out of here—so fucking far away from here.

I blink, and she's gone.

I don't know where she went.

I don't know if she's collapsed behind a bush or tree.

But I have to hold out hope that she's alive. I have to hope my plan can work, that Gage comes through. He's the only one I truly trust. At the moment, I'm not even sure I can trust myself.

21

RI

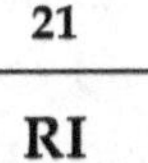

THE WORLD SPINS and spins and spins until I can't make sense of what's up and what's down. I can't differentiate between the stars above and the ground below. I think I'm in a forest of trees, but they spin so quickly I can't figure out where to walk.

There's danger all around. I can sense it, but I can't see it. I don't know where the other men are, but they're here in the forest. I can hear their shouts, their cries of pain, their gunshots. I can hear it all.

The hairs on my arms are standing up, my heart is beating fast with adrenaline, and my body shakes slightly from fear.

I lost Jace and Calvin the second the chaos started. I don't know who shot first, but one second we were trudging through the woods, with Calvin asking me every few minutes if the drugs had kicked in, and the next, there were men everywhere shouting and shooting at us.

It was at that moment I succumbed to the drugs, and everything became foggy. I tried running but couldn't see where I was going; I still can't. I have no hope of surviving if I don't find Jace or Calvin.

I grip my gun tightly, although if a man stood a foot in front of me, I'm not sure if I could tell if they were friend or foe. I rub my hand against my forehead, trying to stop my pounding headache, but it continues to pound.

The spinning doesn't stop either. I don't know what drug I was injected with, but it's a strong one. Thankfully it seems to have mainly just affected my head and not anything else. Everyone else must be in a similar situation.

I take a step forward. Physically I can move just fine. I just need to find Jace or Calvin or at least find a place to hide until the drugs wear off.

I decide my best bet is to crawl low to the ground. I can't tell exactly where bushes or trees are, but I can see blobs of shapes in front of me, so I try to crawl toward those.

Thorns cut into my hand as I crawl on my hands and knees from one of the bushes. I swear under my breath as I fumble to pull a large thorn from the center of my palm.

A nearby gunshot makes my heart jump, and I dive into a thorny bush head first, hoping to be well hidden in the cover of darkness.

The bush's barbs dig in everywhere—my face, hands, knees, hips, fucking everywhere. I bite down on my lip to keep from cursing out in pain as I hear a man walk by, speaking to someone.

I don't recognize either of the voices, so I assume they are my enemies. I hold my breath, trying everything in my power not to move or make a sound until their voices disappear. Only then do I let out a long breath.

Carefully, I roll over onto my back, trying not to inject more spiky thorns into my body, but they are everywhere.

It's going to take me hours to pull all the tiny bristles out. I first focus on the larger thorns to relieve some of my pain.

More men pass, and I freeze once again, holding my breath, but they too move along quickly. My hiding place seems like a good one if four men have now passed me and not spotted me.

My plan was to keep moving, hoping to find Jace and Calvin, but I'm reconsidering my options. It might be better just to stay hidden here, at least until I hear a voice I recognize, or the drugs wear off.

I shiver a little as a cool chill rustles through me, and a drop of rain falls onto my forehead.

I brush it off just as clouds overhead open up and a full-blown rain showers down on top of me.

Fuck.

I won't survive out here all night in the cold rain with no shelter. The ground is already muddy, and the rain just adds to it. Vincent couldn't have planned a better challenge, even if he could control the weather.

If I survive this, if I ever get any real power, I'm going to make Vincent pay for all the suffering he's caused me.

Right now, I have to make a hard decision. Stay in my hiding spot and freeze to death or crawl out and hope to find Jace, Calvin, or shelter.

Neither option is great, but as the rain picks up and my shivering worsens, I decide the better option is to keep moving. I'd rather die from a quick bullet than the slow spiral of hypothermia. And at least if I'm moving, I can pretend I'm doing something to save myself.

Crawling through the thick mud, I have no idea which direction I should be going. Between the drugs and the rain, I can't see anything as mud splashes on my face with each movement.

I move slowly, changing directions when I hear close gunfire. Every time I move away from the sound of people, I'm probably also moving away from finding Jace and Calvin, but it's not safe to move toward the sounds.

The crawling is horrendous. Each movement digs a thorn or branch into some part of my body. I'm sure I'm covered in cuts all over, and I'll be shocked if I don't get an infection from all the mud and dirt trapped in my wounds.

I keep crawling and crawling, knowing if I stand up, I could easily be shot.

Instead of the mud, branches, leaves, bushes, or trees, I expect when I reach my hand forward, this time I feel the unmistakable roughness of a leather boot.

I pull my hand back, terrified to look up at the man I've encountered. I don't know if he's a foe or friend, but the odds aren't in my favor. I'm not even sure if I truly trust Jace or Calvin anyway.

I look up, knowing it's going to be hard for me to make out who it is anyway, expecting to see the end of a gun pointed down at me. The shadow of a man above me is just that—shadows. He seems to sway back and forth, and I can't tell if he's doing that or if my brain is still spinning the world around me.

I narrow my eyes, trying to figure out whom I've stumbled upon. I'm not sure if he's spotted me yet, but the second he takes a step forward and feels my body under his foot, he'll realize it if he hasn't already.

"Snake!" the man yells down at me as he jumps back. "Get away from me, snake!"

I recognize that voice—it's Ryker.

"Ryker, it's me, Ri," I say, slowly standing up with my hands in front of me cautiously.

"You bit me! Get away." He shoots his gun at the ground where I way just lying.

Jesus.

I bite my lip and move behind a tree trunk. Ryker was either injected with a different drug than me, or it affected him differently. He's hallucinating and is no help to me in his current state.

He yells some more—gibberish I can't understand—while I lean against the tree, remaining as still as possible, so he doesn't fire his gun in my direction and hit me on accident.

After a few moments, Ryker moves on. I can still hear him yelling, drawing attention to himself, but he's far enough away that I decide to make a run for it.

This time, I run instead of crawl.

It's hard to dodge the trees, though. I run with my arms outstretched to try and avoid them, but I still hit my hip against the side of a trunk, bruising it badly. I trip on a rock and hit the ground hard a few minutes later, scrambling back to my feet.

After running for five minutes, I feel like I've run far enough to distance myself from Ryker's shrieking. I'm just about to stop when I run into a hard chest.

"Fuck," I let out, knowing there is nowhere to hide this time.

"Thank god," Calvin says.

I exhale a breath of relief.

"I'm so sorry. I can't believe we lost you. There was just gunfire everywhere, and then you were gone," he says.

I shake my head. "Don't be sorry. I'm just glad I found you."

Calvin whistles, and Jace appears a few seconds later next to him.

"I don't think we are far from the house. Can you walk? How do you feel?"

I'm about to answer when something catches my eye—more like someone.

"I can carry you while Calvin carries the case," Jace says.

"No."

"No? Ri, we need to get to the house, then we can get you medical attention. I don't know what the drugs are doing to you, but we ran into Ryker earlier, and he was going ballistic. You aren't right in the right at the moment. You can't make a decision."

"I'm fine."

"But—"

"I ran into Ryker. He's lost it, and he needs your help."

"What? Wasn't James with him? He was following close behind when we ran into him."

I shake my head. "Ryker was on his own, shouting and drawing a lot of attention. You need to find him, or he's dead."

They are both silent for a minute. I'm sure they're considering if they should go save their actual boss or me—a woman they've barely met.

"Jace, go find Ryker. Calvin, take the briefcase to the house and finish the game."

"What about you?" Calvin asks.

"I can hold my own. I injured my leg, so I don't want to slow either of you down. I'll head toward the house on my own."

"But the drugs—"

"Didn't affect me. You were right; mine must have been fake. I'm fine. Go!"

I practically shove them, careful not to show how

much the drugs have, in fact, altered my mental state.

Bullets whizz past us, and neither of them has time to disobey my orders. We all run in different directions. Jace toward Ryker, Calvin toward the house, and me—I dive down on top of Beckett, who is lying far too exposed next to a tree.

I cover him with my body as even more bullets flying overhead. I know I shouldn't. I shouldn't show him that I still have feelings for him. This is the opposite of my plan. My plan was to drive him away and make him hate me. I needed to force him to give up the game—save himself and his men. I wasn't supposed to show I cared, but I can't let him die.

I'd rather die myself than live in a world without him.

A bullet hits the curve of my ear, and I slap a hand over my mouth to keep from crying out. I'm pretty sure I accidentally knee Beckett in the groin when I flail in pain.

"Sorry," I whisper into his ear after I've regained control of myself.

He doesn't say anything in response. At first, I think it's because he's trying to be quiet as not to draw attention to ourselves. But it's strange he hasn't tried to roll me underneath him. He hasn't moved or spoken at all either.

"Try to crawl under that log," I say, lifting myself off of him so he can move without my weight on him.

He doesn't move.

I take slow, deep breaths. I don't know what the drugs have done to him, obviously not the same as to me.

The gunfire stops, and I examine Beckett more carefully. My vision is still shaky, my head still throbs, and the rain still pours, but I can make out Beckett's features. I look over his body, but I don't see any major physical injury.

"Are you hurt?" I plead.

His only answer is a blink of his eyes.

"Move your hand," I say.

I watch his hand, but his fingers barely twitch.

I frown.

He's paralyzed. *Is it the drugs? Is it an injury? Is it permanent?*

I can't think about that now, but I do need some answers.

"Blink once for yes and twice for no. Are you physically injured?"

I wait.

He blinks once, then twice.

I sigh.

"Can you move at all?"

Two blinks—no.

"The drugs did this?"

One blink—yes.

"But mentally, you're still there?"

One blink—yes.

"We can't stay here. We need to find a place to hide until this game is over. Have you seen any of the guys?"

Two blinks—no.

"I'm going to get us to someplace safe. We're sitting ducks out here."

Two blinks—no.

I know why he doesn't want me to help him. I can see it in his eyes. He wants me to save myself, but he'll die if I do. The cold rain, the drugs, or a bullet—any of those could kill him quickly, and I won't allow that to happen.

I don't know what I'm going to do or how I'm going to save us; I just know that I am.

I'm tired of him always doing the saving.

I consider my options for a moment. Dragging him would be slow, and he'd get more injuries from being raked through the mud and brush. He can't hold on at all, so a piggyback ride is out of the question. I can't carry him with just my arms either.

The best way to move him is with a fireman's carry—over my shoulders where his weight is more distributed. But I'm not sure I'm strong enough to lift him into that position.

A loud explosion rattles through us from a distance. The fighting has gotten worse, progressing from just gunfire to full-on bombs being thrown. We have to get out of here. I have to be strong enough.

I bend down into a squatting position and hook my arms under his armpits.

"Push up with your feet if you can."

He moans, and I know he's trying to help. My back strains as I lift with all my might, slowly yanking him up to his feet until he's leaning against my chest.

I hold him there a second, trying to catch my breath before I dip my shoulder underneath him and roll him up across my shoulders. I start moving, fully expecting to collapse from the weight of him soon.

I still can't see worth a damn, but I run anyway, hoping like hell I don't trip and fall.

We bump into a couple of trees along the way, and Beckett gets the worst of the impacts, but somehow he stays on my shoulders as I run. That is until I run almost straight on into a tree. I stumble backward, barely keeping us upright.

"Jesus, Fighter, what's wrong with your sight?" Beckett says.

I gasp with a grin.

22

BECKETT

"You can talk?" Ri asks, flabbergasted.

I'm still on her shoulders, barely able to move, but I have my voice back. For now, I'm more than thankful that I can at least talk.

"I can. I can't move much more than my lips at the moment, though."

She sighs, and her body slumps a little in relief. I feel myself slipping off her back.

"Ri, um, I'm about to fall."

"Oh, sorry." She readjusts my weight, redistributing me on her shoulders.

"I just don't want you to fall because of my dead weight. Although, that seems likely with how you've been running into trees. Is it your vision, or are you physically impaired?"

"Mainly vision. I have a massive headache, and the world seems to be spinning. Are your main symptoms paralysis?"

"Yes, I'm trapped in my body. I can't move. For a while there, I couldn't talk, and I could barely breathe. I've never felt so helpless. And then I saw you, and I couldn't help. I wanted you to run, but I couldn't speak. I couldn't..." my voice cracks, and tears threaten my eyes.

"I couldn't protect you. I couldn't save you. I couldn't even save myself," I finally finish.

There's a long pause between us as we each consider our next words. The last time we were together, it was clear we hated each other, but there is such a fine line between hate and love, between the lies and secrets that hurt and protect us.

I decide to speak first. "But you—you saved me. You risked your life when you could barely see to save me. You shouldn't have saved me; I'm not worth it."

"Maybe I wanted you to owe me a favor," she teases. I can hear the emotion in her voice.

I don't call her out on it. I know why she saved me. She cares, probably even loves me as I love her, but this isn't the time or place to say it. We need to get somewhere safe; we need to find a way out of this nightmare of a game that I started. And if I want Ri, then I have to give up any chance of retribution, even if it means risking my own life in the process.

"We need to move. I have no idea which direction the house is in, but we can't stay exposed to the rain or bullets or bombs. The drugs seem to be affecting everyone differently, so you have no idea how others will react if we run into anyone. And every one that still has full capacities just shoots at any movement they see," she says.

"We need to find some sort of shelter. An abandoned building, a car, a cave, anything," I agree.

"I'll carry you as far as I can," she says.

"You're exhausted, Ri. I'd rather you—"

"No, I'm not putting you down. Not now. Not ever. If

you want to protect me, you can help be my eyes and tell which direction to go, so I don't keep running into trees."

"You're so stubborn."

"I'm not going to leave you to die. You've saved me plenty of times, so it's my turn to save you."

"Fine. Go left; there are fewer trees for you to hit."

I can see her grin out of the corner of my eye as she carries me. It makes me smile too.

She starts walking left, avoiding most of the trees. I just have no idea if we are going to find a place to take shelter.

Rain continues to pelts us, and I can feel her shiver beneath my body from the cold. Her muscles are straining to carry my weight. She'll kill herself trying to carry me; she won't put me down no matter what.

We have to find a safe place to hide soon. I can speak, but that's about all I can do. I can't walk. I can't crawl. My muscles are still entirely paralyzed.

"Tree on your left," I say, and she just barely misses it.

"I'm going to kill Vincent when this is all over. For everything he's put me through, injecting me with a drug like this where I can't fucking see and may have lasting headaches—I'm going to kill him."

She's right, and she should. But I know what she fears most about drugs is her memory being taken away again.

"Any time gaps in your memory?" I ask hesitantly, knowing it could cause her pain, but I need to know.

She doesn't answer immediately, probably trying to assess her own memory. "No, I don't think so. But it's hard to tell sometimes until someone asks me something, and I have no recollection of it."

"I'll be here for you no matter what."

Thunder roars in the distance ominously. I can't keep letting her carry me much longer.

"There!" I say suddenly.

"What?"

"There's a small cave, down and to your right."

She follows my lead, and the second we enter the cave, she collapses. I try with everything in me to roll off her, but I can't.

"Ri, are you okay? Talk to me. Am I crushing you?"

She laughs. "I'm fine. Just exhausted."

"Roll me off you."

"No, I like feeling your body against mine, and you're keeping me warm."

I sigh. "Ri, please."

She laughs and rolls me off her back with a thud. She pushes up on her elbows to get a better look at me.

She frowns. "I wish I could see you better."

"I wish I could reach out and touch you."

She gasps loudly and looks away suddenly, hiding the emotions on her face. When she turns back, she's stone-faced.

"This doesn't change anything. Just because I saved you doesn't mean anything. I'm pissed at you, and you're pissed at me. Neither of us wants to share our secrets. We aren't on the same team."

"Sure, whatever you say, Fighter."

"Don't call me that."

I grin. "Why not?"

She looks at me intensely. "You know why not."

I take a deep, painful breath. "Stop fighting it."

"I can't. I can't risk getting hurt, especially by you." She shivers.

I hate that I can't warm her. "Dammit, how long until these drugs wear off?"

She shrugs. "My guess would be sometime tomorrow."

I can't sit here and watch her freeze all night while I do nothing.

"Take off my clothes. Then get naked."

"What? Why?" she pants.

"We need to get these wet clothes off and warm up with our body heat."

She blushes. I can see it even beneath the thick layers of mud stuck to her skin.

"You're beautiful and strong and carried me half a mile to safety. Don't you get bashful on me now, Fighter."

She chuckles as she crawls over to me and begins to take off my boots. "I just didn't think I'd ever be naked again with you after last time."

She moves to the buttons on my jeans and then begins shimming my pants down my hips. I try to lift my legs to help, but I barely move a muscle. She removes my pants, my underwear, and my shirt like a skilled nurse taking care of me. Her gaze avoids all the areas she usually most enjoys. She's matter of fact as she undresses me.

Then she stands and turns away from me as she removes her own clothes.

"Look away," she says with her back to me.

I divert my eyes, and she launches herself at me, curling up next to my naked body, tucking herself under my arm, being as modest as she possibly can be.

"Fighter," I breathe.

"Yes?"

"I can't move. I sure as hell can't fuck you. You can snuggle with me however you want to stay warm."

"I know. I just…"

"What?"

She finally looks at me. She can't see much at the

moment because of the drugs, but she studies my face, and I know she can see plenty.

"Can I kiss you?" she asks, her voice so quiet I think I imagined it.

"Always."

She presses her lips against mine. It's the one part of my body I can control, the only part I can use to show her exactly how I feel.

The second our lips touch, I'm hers. Everything clicks into place in my brain as well as my heart. I see what I've been missing all this time, more clearly now than before.

Our tongues swirl around each other's mouths, deepening the kiss as far as it can go. For a second, I'm glad all I can do is kiss her. If I could fuck her, I wouldn't want to fall into old patterns of making it feel like a goodbye. The next time I fuck her, I want it to be the start of a lifetime of sex, not like the end.

This kiss feels like the start of something, both of us pouring our feelings into the kiss. For once, both of us share the exact same feeling.

I love you.

That's what we say with the kisses over and over and over.

Each lap of our tongues.

Each moan in our throats.

Each tug of our lips.

All of it is telling the other how much we love them.

Uncontrollably, she ends our kiss with a yawn against my lips, and I can tell how exhausted she is. I want to tell her my feelings. I want to tell her everything. I want to ask her all my questions because I think for once she'd actually answer them. But right now, sleep is more important.

"Sleep, Fighter."

She yawns again with a smile, and this time, she wraps herself fully around me, pulling my arm around her body. Soon, she's asleep, and I enjoy watching her. My hand rests on her stomach, and for a long time, I focus on making my hand move. I plead with my hand to comfort her in some way, knowing that being able to move is the only thing I can do to protect her.

After what seems like hours, I'm finally able to move my thumb, then more of my fingers, and finally my entire hand. I rub up and down her smooth skin as she sleeps against my chest. Only then do I close my eyes and try to sleep.

I don't know what tomorrow will bring.

I had a plan. I thought I was in full control, knowing what I was doing. I'm no longer sure how to save us both, but I know whom I'll choose to save if it comes to it.

23

RI

I WAKE up curled around a naked Beckett. His hand rubs up and down my back soothingly as he smiles up at me.

"Wait...you can move," I practically scream.

"I can. And you?"

I blink rapidly, but there is no cloudiness to my vision, no dizziness, just a mild headache.

"I can see. No more bumping into trees."

He grabs the back of my head and pulls me into a kiss sending delicious little shockwaves through my body. "Thank god for that."

My gaze goes up and down his body. I lick my lips as I think of all the dirty things I want to do with him.

"Down, girl. We aren't in a safe place yet. We need to get out of here."

I sigh and roll off of him.

We both quickly put our clothes back on. They're only slightly less damp than when we removed them last night. We both grip our guns as we stand at the edge of the cave.

"What's the plan?" I ask.

"We get out the woods, find a car, and drive as far away from all of this as we can."

"We don't go back to Caius's place?"

"No. We need to get away from everyone. Then we can figure out a plan."

I blink, not sure I believe what I'm hearing. It sounds like Beckett is ready to fight for us, for our future. He'll fight with me to put an end to Vincent's game. He'll find a way for us to be together.

Now isn't the time to talk about it, though.

"Ready?" I ask.

He nods.

We head out of the cave into the early sunrise. We're cautious at first, listening carefully for any sounds of others still lurking. But other than a few birds chirping, we don't hear much.

Still, we are silent as we walk, so we don't draw any unwanted attention our way.

In the light of day, we are able to see footprints in the mud. Beckett remembers where the cars were parked, so we trudge in that direction.

After walking for a bit, Beckett stops.

"Hop on my back."

I frown. "No, I can walk."

"I know you can, but you carried me last night, and I can tell you're hurting. Let me help you."

My back is killing me, and my legs barely want to move anymore.

"Fine," I grumble as I climb on Beckett's back.

He seems to carry me easily as he walks out of the forest. I must admit I enjoy it—being a lot closer to him, being able to smell him and feel the muscles moving in his back.

We continue on like that for at least an hour before finally coming to a clearing.

"There's a car still here," I sigh in relief. Beckett gently sets me down on the ground.

"You know how to hotwire a car?"

"Of course, do you?"

He winks at me, and we both jog over to the car. It turns out we don't have to hotwire it, as the keys are already inside.

We hop in quickly, and Beckett floors it.

I lean my head back against the headrest. "God, how did we survive that?"

"Because you're the most fucking incredible woman, that's why."

I smile over at him. "It was rhetorical."

I'm about to ask what the plan is when a car pulls out in front of us suddenly. Beckett slams on the brakes to avoid hitting the car, but our abrupt stop sets the airbags off.

My head spins a little from the sudden stop.

"Beckett, are you—" I don't get my words out as I'm ripped from the car.

At first, I think it might be a Good Samaritan who saw us stop suddenly and is trying to help us. But from the way I'm roughly being gripped and my arms tugged behind my back, I'm being kidnapped, not saved.

"Beckett!" I yell, but I don't see him. Is he still in the car, or did they already drag him out?

I try to shake the men off, but I can't. My wrists are already tied behind my back. My gun has been taken. I'm not going to be able to fight them off.

"Don't hurt him! I'll do whatever you want; just don't hurt him!" I scream.

There are chuckles all around me.

Goosebumps creep up my spine. Finally, I look up into the faces of my captors.

Caius.

Gage.

Lennox.

Hayes.

And even more men, all of whom I assume belong to the Retribution Kings.

My heart drops.

I've been played. Beckett took advantage of my emotions and got me to trust him. He set me up; I just don't know why.

———

I wasn't drugged; that's the only thing I can be thankful for. They bound my hands and ankles. They gagged me. They threw me in the back of a van and didn't speak to me.

Now I'm being carried by men I thought I could trust. Men I thought were on my side. Men I thought were good and decent.

This doesn't make any sense. I'm usually a good judge of character, and I still think I am.

So why are they treating me like I'm the enemy? What am I missing?

Hayes has a look of concern on his face as he carries me. Lennox keeps glancing back at me like he can't believe what's happening. Gage refuses to look back at me, and Caius is chewing on his bottom lip like he's about to bite it off.

We enter the building on the Retribution King's

complex where Caius and Beckett fought. I still haven't seen any sign of Beckett.

The only thing I'm hoping for is that this is some sort of initiation. That Beckett has chosen me as his new bride, and this is some weird part of a tradition they have to do. Kidnap me to ensure I'm strong enough for him or something. Judging by the serious looks on all the guys' faces, that's not the case.

Hayes carries me while the others guard me from all sides as we walk into the building, up the stairs, and to the stage in the center of the room.

People are already seated like they are waiting for play. It feels more like I'm being carried to my execution, and I have no idea what I did to deserve this.

When we get to the stage, I see a pole has been bolted to the floor. I look into Hayes's eyes, begging him to stop this. Don't tie me to that pole; run and get me out of here.

He doesn't look at me, but I can feel his heart racing a million miles a minute when my head falls against his chest.

Something's wrong—very, very wrong.

Hayes stops in front of the pole, and all the guys face us now. My arms are undone from behind my back but are immediately tied together above my head and then to a chain attached to the top of the pole.

I'm still gagged. My ankles are tied together. I'm covered in mud, and my clothes are still wet from last night.

I can't do much about my appearance, but I won't appear weak. I look out into the crowd of people that are obviously here to watch something involving me. I won't show fear. I will stare every one of them down if I have to.

Caius picks up a microphone and starts speaking. "As

you all know, we are here today to finish the initiation of Beckett Monroe into our ranks. After today, there will be no doubt that he is our leader. He was given the final task of getting retribution for Odette's death. And today, he's figured out who caused my sister's death."

The room is silent as my heart beats wildly in my chest.

"Beckett, if you will, please come to the stage."

Beckett walks up the same steps I was just carried up. Unlike me, he isn't covered in mud and wet clothes. He's showered and is wearing dark jeans and a grey shirt. He doesn't look at me; he walks to Caius's side.

"Would you like to show the evidence on Odette's killer?" Caius asks.

Beckett nods. "Play the video."

I turn my head to see a screen coming down behind me, and then a video starts playing. It takes me no time at all to realize it's footage of the night Odette was taken. What shocks me is that scene of me or a woman who looks very much like me, walking into the room.

My heart stops as I realize why I'm here. I'm the retribution. They've brought me here because they blame me for Odette's death. And Beckett is about to kill me in order to get revenge for his wife.

I watch the video.

I watch myself stab Odette.

None of it rings any bells.

It's a blank space in my memory.

But there are so many confusing things about this video beyond not remembering doing it. For one, Odette's wounds are all extremely superficial for the amount of blood I know is left in the room. For two, I'm not fighting in the way I usually would. And three, I would never fight an innocent woman.

Is this really me?

The woman who looks like me turns, and there's a scar under her ear—a scar that I have.

It's me.

But why?

I can't make sense of it.

The video stops.

Beckett takes the microphone. "The evidence speaks for itself."

The crowd nods and shouts their agreement.

"The price Rialta Corsi will pay for killing Odette is her life," Beckett continues.

The crowd cheers. They cheer my death like I'm a monster. I guess to them, I am. I'm the woman who killed their princess. I deserve to die.

Beckett hands Caius the microphone, and then he walks to me. His steps are slow, strong, majestic. I'm mesmerized by how powerful he looks as he walks toward me. He's going to take my life without a word.

I'm stunned into silence. There is nothing I can do. I can't speak. I can't move. I can't fight for my life.

All I can do is look Beckett in his eyes and plead with him, try to make him realize that I didn't do this. This isn't me; he has to believe me.

I love him. I would never hurt his wife. I would never kill anyone innocent.

He walks about a foot away from me, and then he stops suddenly. That's when I notice the gun in his hand.

At least it will be a quick death.

I don't want to appear afraid, but the tiniest of tears

escapes the corner of my eye. Not because I'm about to die, maybe this will be for the best. My father can't marry me off if I'm dead. No, I shed a tear because I thought he loved me. Last night, I truly thought he did.

I was wrong.

He hates me.

I close my eyes before he can raise the gun to kill me. Even though he'll be the reason I die, I don't want to die thinking he hates me. I want the memories of last night in that cave to fill me as I leave this earth.

"Wait!" A high-pitched voice rings out. "Wait! Don't do it!"

A hush comes over the crowd, and I finally open my eyes. Every man on stage has drawn their gun and is staring at the stairs where a blonde woman is running up them.

No one moves.

No one speaks.

All eyes are on this woman.

I can't quite see who it is until she reaches the stage, but she comes into view, and there is no doubt who it is.

Her long thin legs, bouncing blonde hair, and thick red lips. A spitting image of the woman I just watched myself stab on video.

It can't be.

She's dead.

And yet, Odette Monroe stands in front of us all.

Beckett can't tear his eyes away from her. He looks like he's seen a ghost—we all have.

"Don't...don't shoot," she sobs, walking to Beckett and taking his hand like he's hers. "Rialta didn't kill me. She helped me escape."

Did I help her? I don't remember this woman. I don't remember anything.

I still can't get over how undead she is; she's very much alive.

That means Beckett won't kill me in retribution.

It means he's still married to her.

It means my heart is breaking into a thousand pieces.

Odette is still gripping Beckett's hand like long lost lover. She must see pity in my eyes because she bends down and whispers in my ear. A single phrase is spoken from her lips, and all my memories return.

A lot of things now make sense, and yet looking at Beckett, knowing that he was about to kill me, none of it matters.

I just lost the only man I've ever loved.

———

Thank you for reading Tempted Hero! I hope you enjoyed it! Beckett and Ri's story continues in Fatal Princess!

ALSO BY ELLA MILES

LIES SERIES:

Lies We Share: A Prologue

Vicious Lies

Desperate Lies

Fated Lies

Cruel Lies

Dangerous Lies

Endless Lies

SINFUL TRUTHS:

Sinful Truth #1

Twisted Vow #2

Reckless Fall #3

Tangled Promise #4

Fallen Love #5

Broken Anchor #6

TRUTH OR LIES:

Taken by Lies #1

Betrayed by Truths #2

Trapped by Lies #3

Stolen by Truths #4

Possessed by Lies #5

Consumed by Truths #6

DIRTY SERIES:

Dirty Obsession

Dirty Addiction

Dirty Revenge

Dirty: The Complete Series

ALIGNED SERIES:

Aligned: Volume 1 (Free Series Starter)

Aligned: Volume 2

Aligned: Volume 3

Aligned: Volume 4

Aligned: The Complete Series Boxset

UNFORGIVABLE SERIES:

Heart of a Thief

Heart of a Liar

Heart of a Prick

Unforgivable: The Complete Series Boxset

MAYBE, DEFINITELY SERIES:

Maybe Yes

Maybe Never

Maybe Always

Definitely Yes

Definitely No

Definitely Forever

STANDALONES:

Pretend I'm Yours

Pretend We're Over

Finding Perfect

Savage Love

Too Much

Not Sorry

Hate Me or Love Me: An Enemies to Lovers Romance Collection

ABOUT THE AUTHOR

Ella Miles writes steamy romance, including everything from dark suspense romance that will leave you on the edge of your seat to contemporary romance that will leave you laughing out loud or crying. Most importantly, she wants you to feel everything her characters feel as you read.

Ella is currently living her own happily ever after near the Rocky Mountains with her high school sweetheart husband. Her heart is also taken by her goofy five year old black lab who is scared of everything, including her own shadow.

Ella is a USA Today Bestselling Author & Top 50 Bestselling Author.

Stalk Ella at:
www.ellamiles.com
ella@ellamiles.com